Short Stories to Inspire & Delight

edited by

Elaine Leet

Musings

Short Stories to Inspire & Delight

For permission requests, write to the publisher, addressed
"Attention: Permissions Coordinator,"
stonebearpub@gmail.com

Quantity sales special discounts are available on quantity purchases by corporations, associations, and others. For details, contact the publisher at
stonebearpub@gmail.com

Book Layout & Cover Design - DBree, StoneBear Design

Manufactured and printed in the United States of America

ISBN: 978-1-957883-11-3 Paperback
ISBN: 978-1-957883-12-0 eBook
Library of Congress Control Number: 2023904202

STONEBEAR™
PUBLISHING

stonebearpublishing.com

Introduction

THE SECOND DECADE OF THE 21ST CENTURY STARTED with lots of "me time." That added time for thought and reflection led me to one inescapable conclusion: I'm not entirely satisfied with the way things are going. I'm not talking about the lack of flying cars, extraterrestrial visitations, or transporter beams. I'm referring to the way people tend to stay stuck in discontent even though we have the resources to try for something better.

Thanks to our technology, we have unprecedented access to information. We don't bat an eye at first hand reports and live video from almost anywhere on Earth or from orbit around the planet or even Mars. We can find almost anybody's erudite opinion on just about anything posted on social media. The trick is to sort the pertinent facts from the misinformation, disinformation, and outright lies. Only when we accept the accuracy of the information, can we add it to our knowledge.

Then there is experience. Experience can be a hard teacher. Getting experience and developing judgment can make us look the fool. It can freak us out. It can be expensive. It can destroy trust in ourselves and others.

Even more challenging than experience is reflection that puts the information and knowledge in context and pulls from it the guiding principles that prompt better choices. Choices that benefit ourselves and others.

In this collection of stories are examples of characters drawing on wisdom to embark on new beginnings. Some characters encounter situations that offer new perspectives. Others draw on knowing themselves to recognize the wisdom of taking a new direction.

I hope you enjoy these stories.

I hope you take that risk and launch yourself into daring new beginnings.

Dedication

This book is dedicated to You,

the ones who

took a chance and bought our book,

laughed at our funnies,

nodded in recognition of wisdom that matches your own,

tilted your heads at a new idea,

and

shed a tear empathizing with a character.

Thank you!

CONTENTS

Marylou Webster Ambrose
BlowUp

YESTERDAY, MY SEVENTEEN-YEAR-OLD SON told me he plans to apply for a job delivering pizzas. Most fathers would be proud. Me? My life flashed before my eyes. Actually, not my whole life, just one night when I was his age and delivering pizzas. I never told anyone about this, but maybe now's the time . . .

I was driving a red '84 Chevy Cavalier, my first car. It was a convertible, and the roof leaked when it rained. But there wasn't room in the garage for it, and I didn't have money for a cover. So a lot of the time, I sat on garbage bags so my butt wouldn't get wet.

My summer job was delivering pizzas for Tony's Trattoria. I made minimum wage—$4.25 an hour in those days. But usually, the tips made up for it. There were three Italian restaurants in the area, but Tony's was the only one that delivered. The weekenders from New York and New Jersey were used to ordering in, so they were our best customers.

The backseat was folded down, and six large pizzas were sitting behind me in an insulated bag. I checked the list, and all my deliveries were within a ten-mile radius. Two went to an address in Englewood Lakes, a big development; two went to a rental cottage on Lake Lenape; and two went to a house in the town of Hailey.

I was sailing along with the top down, sitting on a plastic bag, feeling pretty good because I'd just smoked part of a joint. It was a Saturday night, getting dark, and I figured the people I was delivering to must be having parties, because it was too late for dinner. I'd already delivered another carload at dinner time, and this was my last run for the night.

The radio was turned up and 2 Unlimited was rapping "The Twilight

Zone." I had to laugh, because my dad loved that old TV show with the same name, and whenever something weirded him out, he'd start singing the lame theme song, like "dodododododododo." He'd made me watch the show with him a few times, and it was actually pretty cool, especially the episode with the doll that says it's gonna kill you.

Anyway, I was cruising along, bopping my head to the music and drumming my hand on the steering wheel. I was the only car on Route 5, which was odd for a weekend night. I pulled my ball cap tighter on my head so I wouldn't lose it in the wind and enjoyed the scenery whizzing by: trees, cottages, a glimpse of the lake on the right.

I swung a left into the entrance to Englewood Lakes and slowed down. The security idiots in these developments liked to nab you for speeding. I squinted at the bill from Tony's to find the address: 124 Westbrook Avenue. I knew where it was because I'd delivered there before. The road was right off the main drag and a few houses down. The driveway was full, so I parked on the road. I unzipped the heating bag in the back and slid out the top two pizzas: one cheese-only and the other sausage and pepperoni.

Walking toward the house, cradling the warm pizzas, I got a funny feeling. Maybe it was just the pot I'd smoked, but the smell of sauce, cheese, and meat drifting through the cardboard made my stomach do a flip-flop. Then I burped and threw up in my throat. I hated when that happened. I stopped, swallowed hard, took a couple deep breaths, and tightened my grip on the pizza boxes. Shit, suppose I'd dropped them? I was feeling better, so I finished walking to the front door and rang the bell.

A few seconds later, the door opened and a woman my mom's age stood there, dressed in one of those fringed flapper outfits. I could hear people laughing inside the house. The woman giggled. "We're having a Roaring '20s murder mystery party," she explained. "I guess they didn't eat pizza then, but who cares?"

She put the pizza boxes on a table while we settled up the money. She had exact change, which made it easy. Then she gave me a two-buck tip and closed the door, and that was that. I turned and walked back down the driveway, got in my car, and headed to my next customer. My stomach had calmed down, but now my head felt funny. I wondered if I should lay off the weed for a while, at least when I was driving.

Turning left onto Route 5, I headed for Lake Lenape, this dinky lake with a bunch of overpriced houses around the perimeter. The customer was at the beginning of the road in one of the rental cottages. The name on the bill was Ploranski. Probably some dude from Jersey up for the weekend. The store down the road got so sick of these guys complaining about their bagels and stuff, they put up a sign that said, "We don't care how you make it in New Jersey."

I hoped they wouldn't complain about the pizza. Didn't matter, though, because I'd be out of there before that happened.

I turned right onto the private road, then made a quick left into the cottages. They weren't numbered—none of the houses on this road were—but the customer had said it was the third one on the left. I counted one, two, three, found it, parked, went through the same routine with the zippered bag in the back seat, and headed for the door. I balanced the pizzas in my left hand and lifted my right hand to knock. But before my knuckles hit the door, a voice behind me said, "Don't."

I jerked around, felt the pizza boxes shift in my left arm, and grabbed them with my other hand before they could fall. Whew! Close call. There was no one behind me. But I swear I had heard a voice. Then the door opened and a guy in gym shorts and a black Evil Dead T-shirt was leaning there with a big smile on his face.

"You're just in time," he said, stepping aside so I could enter.

Except I didn't want to. Something felt off, had felt off all night. My feet wouldn't move, and I stood there like an asshole, holding the pizzas. The guy kept grinning. "Pizza's here," he called over his shoulder. Then he turned back to me and said, "Party's just starting. Sure you don't wanna come in?"

I looked past him and saw his friends sitting on the couch. Three guys in shorts and T-shirts. And four naked women with their red mouths wide open. Wait—holy shit, those were blow-up dolls!

The guy kept on grinning. Then he grabbed my upper arm and yanked. I wrenched away and the pizza boxes landed on the floor. I tripped over my feet running back to the car and jumped in like some kind of clumsy action hero without even opening the door. Luckily, my keys were still in the ignition. I heard raucous laughter as I peeled out of there like the devil was chasing me—and maybe he was.

I sped down Route 5, blubbering like a baby. I don't know how far I drove before I realized I was going the wrong way. My last delivery was in the opposite direction. I calmed down enough to pull into the parking lot of the Methodist church. I figured I'd sit there until my heart stopped hammering. Maybe even pray a little. Tomorrow this would all seem funny. My buddies would get a big kick out of it.

I leaned back in the seat, took a deep breath, and looked up at the starless sky. Something touched my neck and said, "I'm hungry." I whipped around and saw a red, open mouth—and screamed.

The sky was just turning pink when I came to. What was I doing in the church parking lot? Then it all came back to me and I scrambled out of the car, breathing hard. The back seat was empty. Even the insulated bag was gone. But whoever, or whatever, had been in my back seat had left me a ten-dollar tip.

###

This story first appeared in Reedsy Contest #140, under the writing prompt: Write a story that involves a flashback.

Visit https://blog.reedsy.com/creative-writing-prompts.

Laurie A. Guzda

The Bump & Grind

LIA SAT IN THE BUMP & GRIND, sipping her cappuccino while finishing her Medium article on "How to Write for Medium." She had a decent following. Between that and her several other platforms, Lia was able to generate enough revenue through her writing to cover monthly expenses—barely. She had a pilot under consideration at Netflix.

She had more time to write these days, having recently ended a three-year relationship with Marco. Marco the wandering cock, as her friends referred to him. Lia was blindsided by his deceit. At thirty-two, her biological clock was ticking loudly. Maybe she didn't want to see the truth. Regardless, now she was alone, wrapped in her blanket of distrust, focused on what she loved most: people-watching and writing. "Living life from a distance," Lia muttered to no one.

A beautiful woman sat at the next table, in conversation on her phone. Lia couldn't help but overhear her talking about the man she was soon meeting. It was an online dating meet. The woman said that he seemed nice but desperate. When the man approached the table, the woman quickly ended the call. She gave him a forced, fake smile through recently pumped up lips.

Lia tried to write. She tried not to eavesdrop, but she couldn't help herself. She listened to the entire conversation. The woman was a model . . . grew up on a farm . . . an only child who hated living in the city. The man made a sound as if to speak, but she ignored him. She sounded like she wanted to cry because she thought people were mean and insensitive to her needs. Then she brightened talking about how she wanted to change the world and wondered why we couldn't just have world peace. She blamed the people of the Middle East and Texas.

The man never had a chance to speak. He tried to ask questions, but the woman rambled on. Lia wondered if she was bipolar. She glanced over and saw the man stifle a yawn. When the brief encounter ended, it was obvious both he and the woman were relieved. And that's why I don't do online dating, Lia thought as she packed up her computer.

It was two o'clock, and Lia was already late for her appointment at the senior living community. She was helping her grandmother, Gigi, create a comedy sketch for their fundraiser variety show. Gigi had a better social life than Lia did. Her ability to socialize gracefully was to be envied. And lord knows the woman still had moves. Lia looked like a broken, empty Pez dispenser when she danced.

Gigi, Mr. Carpenter, Miss Susie, and Bad Scott were all waiting for Lia when she arrived. "I'm sorry I'm late, but I've written something for your show." Lia handed out scripts. "I was thinking we could do a spoof on your nursing home."

"It's a senior living community," snorted Bad Scott. There were two Scotts living in the building, and obviously this was not the good one.

"Well, now it's the Stairway to Heaven Assisted Living Commune." Lia smiled as she continued. "The idea is that you've all returned to Woodstock for the seventy-fifth anniversary."

"A Woodstock reunion! I love it!" Gigi roared.

"I still have an afro wig from when we did Hair," said Miss Susie, who would play the stoner hippie chick.

Gigi said, "I have the perfect flowing, flowered robe for the exotic psychic, Natasha."

Bad Scott, cast as the miserable militant Sarge, simply grunted. And Mr. Carpenter would play the hefty and happy, yet somewhat forgetful, Farmer Yaz. He was proud that he still owned his well-worn overalls from the 1960s.

After they finished the read-through, Lia began gathering her belongings. She said, "I think that's enough for today. Learn your lines so we can start blocking." She got up to leave, and Gigi walked her to the door.

"There's a new doctor on staff that I think you should meet."

"Why? I'm not sick," replied Lia. Then she softened and said, "I'm not ready, Gigi. I'm terrible at dating. You know I'd do anything for you, and I appreciate your concern, but I don't like being set up. For me, it needs to be organic. I need to look into someone's eyes and see them, really see them. You know what I mean?"

"I understand. Just think about it, OK?" Gigi kissed Lia's forehead and returned to her friends, who were laughing over the script.

Lia stopped at the door and turned back to the group. She loved the sound of their laughter.

A few days later, Lia called her agent. "Hey, Barb, it's Lia Sanford checking in. Have you heard anything from Netflix?"

"They're not saying no, but they're not saying yes. They really want children's shows. Can you revise it?" Barb asked.

"Sure, I mean what's more interesting than a twelve-year-old venture capitalist?" Lia couldn't suppress her sarcasm.

"A twelve-year-old navigating a start-up is a great concept," Barb encouraged.

"Okay, should I substitute cocaine with sugar and turn the orgy into a play date?"

Barb laughed. "They really are the same thing; might as well prepare these kids from the get-go. Hang in there, kid. Talk later."

Lia was sipping her coffee in the Bump & Grind when she noticed the hapless guy from the other day sitting in the corner. He looked like he was waiting for another date. He's either persistent, a glutton for punishment, or a pervert, Lia thought.

A woman wearing a cowboy hat burst in the front door. "Gary? Is there a Gary here?" The man in the corner looked wide-eyed and appalled. He barely raised his hand to acknowledge that he was, indeed, the aforementioned Gary. Lia watched the woman leap to his table, then grab a chair and turn it around to sit. With her legs spread wide and arms crossed along the rim of the chair back, she just looked at Gary with a slight smile and squinted eyes.

"Well ain't you a handsome plate of meat," the woman's southern drawl announced loud enough for everyone in the coffee shop to hear.

Oh my god, did she just say that? Lia was embarrassed for the man. He tried to lower the volume of the conversation as he leaned over to shake hands with the woman. But she was having none of it. She ranted about riding hard and cattle prods. He pulled his phone out of his pocket, read something, stood, and reached his hand out again.

"An emergency? No, baby, we're just getting started. OK, call me when you're done." Miss Southern's gaze followed Gary as he walked out the door. Then her eyes locked onto another man at a nearby table. She stood and walked toward him. Realizing she was gunning for him, the man stood, knocked over his chair, and ran out before she could reach him.

A week later, Gary was sitting across from yet another woman in the Bump & Grind. They appeared to be having a polite conversation, although the woman seemed nervous as she shoveled cake into her mouth. Suddenly, her face began to swell and broke out in bright red blotches, her eyes becoming slits. "Are you OK?" asked Gary.

"Oh no, there must be nuts in the cake! I'm bweafy awergic."

"Do you have an EpiPen?" he asked. She shook her head no.

Gary called 911. The ambulance arrived, and EMTs quickly strapped the woman onto the gurney.

Lia looked at her watch and realized she had to leave for rehearsal. Just as she stood and turned to exit, the EMTs pushed her aside as they bounded out of the coffee shop with the patient. Gary was following alongside the gurney.

The EMTs were struggling with the door. Lia looked at the swollen woman and then up to Gary. "Another date, huh?" They finally managed to get the stretcher into the ambulance. It drove off, leaving Gary watching from the sidewalk.

Back at the senior living community, Lia started rehearsal. "Let's pick it up with your lines, Mr. Carpenter. Start with 'I get by with a little help from Depends.'"

Bad Scott interrupted. "What about me?"

He was unhappy. "Miss Susie is the healer, Gigi is the psychic, and Mr. Carpenter is the farmer. What am I supposed to be?"

"Okay, how about you be the pool boy? You're in charge of recreation."

"Oh boy! I'm the pool boy!" Bad Scott went off to work on his lines.

"All right, Mr. Carpenter, let's go back to your announcement."

Mr. Carpenter, in his overalls, tie-dyed shirt, full beard, bandanna headband, and granny glasses, grabbed the microphone and enthusiastically began reciting his lines.

"I have a message here for Irving Glucksman to call home. Use your cell. Ask someone to help you. Just flip it open and dial. Your kids have issued a silver alert. So call right away and let them know you're OK." He stopped and looked to Lia for approval. The others laughed.

They were having so much fun.

The next day, back at the Bump & Grind, Lia was finishing an article when she looked up to see Gary standing in front of her. "May I help you?"

"I . . . um . . . I . . . ah, I just wanted to say hello," stammered Gary. "I've seen you here a few times and just wanted to introduce myself. I'm Gary."

"Yes, I've seen you too." In an exaggerated southern accent Lia added, "Why, y'all is a mighty fine plate of meat."

Gary, embarrassed, replied, "Yes, that would be me. I'm sorry, I didn't mean to intrude. I'm just trying to make friends. I'm new around here."

"Oh, I see. It must be hard, especially when the last one left on a stretcher," Lia offered with a forced smile.

"Sorry to have bothered you." Gary walked away.

What a weirdo, Lia thought.

Meanwhile, back at the senior living community, Bad Scott had acquired a pool skimmer and brandished it, nearly hitting Miss Susie in the face. She grabbed the pole and admonished him nose-to-nose: "I swear to god, this pole is going to be cleaning your colon if you're not careful."

"But I'm the pool boy. I need my prop," begged Bad Scott.

Miss Susie unscrewed the mesh head of the skimmer and handed that back to him. "Here's your prop, pool boy."

Mr. Carpenter continued on stage as the emcee: "We've got some sponsors to thank for helping to make Woodstock '75 a reality. Piece of My Heart Cardiology Group and Artificial Hippie Hip Replacement Boutique Clinic. A special thanks to the Stairway to Heaven Assisted Living Commune for hosting this event. And the new cemetery, the Velvet Underground, who is partnering with Sly and the Family Headstone to offer a 10 percent discount when your show your ticket stub."

Gigi sat next to Lia. She put a hand on her hand. "Thank you for helping us. It's a very funny sketch. And we're having so much fun doing this. I think you're an excellent writer and director." And in her best Russian accent, wearing her flowing, flowered robe, she added, "I predict this vill be best show ever." They laughed.

Later that day, Barb called to say Netflix had passed on Lia's pilot. "But don't worry—Paramount and Hulu are desperate for material." Lia knew she should be used to rejection by now, but she sank into the black hole of despair anyway. One rejection spiraled into everything becoming meaningless. What made her think she could write?

The next morning, Lia sat in the Bump & Grind writing an article about the emotional pitfalls of being a writer. She was in the zone as her fingers flew over the keys banging out words. She felt someone sit behind her on the long bench seat but kept writing. She wrote and wrote until, like a car running out of gas, she sputtered until she was empty. When she stopped to reread what she'd just written, her ears perked up at a familiar voice. It was Gary.

For the first time, she realized another man was sitting with Gary, and that Gary was pouring his heart out. "I know it's been three years since Cathy died. And she was sick for three years before that. I get it—I need to move on. I miss her, but I really do want to move on. I took this job for that very reason. But it's just so hard to meet people. You're my only friend in this city, and I've been here for six months. I'm not doing any more ridiculous online dating. I need to feel a connection. I just want someone I can talk to, that I can laugh with. I need to look into someone's eyes and feel them." The other man responded as their conversation continued in a low, somber tone.

Lia felt a tear slide down her cheek. She felt horrible. How could she have been so wrong in judging Gary? Why must she always judge? Why couldn't they be friends? Shame on me. How could I have been so rude? She wiped her eyes and turned to speak with him, but he was already walking out the door.

A week later, applause thundered from the crowded community room at the senior living center. It was intermission. As Lia stood near the table filled with homemade baked goods, Gigi came up from behind. "Oh Lia, look at the great turnout. We've raised over two thousand dollars for our community fund, and that's not including food and coffee."

"It's a fun show. Are you guys ready? When do you go on?"

"We're the closing act! Always leave 'em laughing, right? Oh, Lia, I want you to meet Dr. Goodman." Gigi called to a gentleman with his back to them. He turned and Lia gasped. It was Gary.

When he saw Gigi, he smiled a big grin, but it quickly disappeared when he saw Lia. Gary and Lia stood and looked at each other. "Do you two know each other?" asked a surprised and somewhat confused Gigi.

"Kinda," Lia said to Gigi, and then she turned to Gary and held out her hand. "I'm Lia Sanford, Gigi's granddaughter."

Gary politely shook her hand. "Nice to meet you," they both said flatly in unison.

Gigi gave them a strange look. "I've got to get backstage. I'll see you kids after the show." She hurried away.

Lia felt awkward as she stood next to Gary, and she knew he felt the same. As the show resumed, she watched him out of the corner of her eye. She wanted to say something, but what? How to apologize? She couldn't help but notice what a beautiful profile he had. Nice full lips. Lia liked full lips. She liked his ears. He had cute ears. She turned her attention back to a woman reading poetry on stage.

Lia noticed Gary sneaking a look at her, but he didn't say anything, either. Probably afraid I'll say something sarcastic, she thought.

Then it was time for the finale. Gigi and Miss Susie were singing "Tommy can you hear me? Tommy, can you hear me? Tommy? Turn on, man . . . turn on your hearing aids and tune out." The audience burst out laughing.

Mr. Carpenter was thanking the sponsors when Bad Scott came out, pool skimmer head in hand, and grabbed the microphone, adding, "Watch out for the bad acid reflux medicine that's going around."

By time they finished, the audience was on its feet giving them a standing ovation. Gary was clapping loudly and still laughing. He looked at Lia. "That was great. That's the most I've laughed in a long time."

They stood looking at each other. Lia looked deep into Gary's soulful eyes and saw him, really saw him. Gary looked into Lia's eyes and she thought he felt her, really felt her.

"You know, rumor has it that you're a good coffee date," she said with a sly smile.

Gary smiled back. "Tomorrow? The Bump & Grind?"

"Absolutely."

.

.

Donna Consiglio

Coyote and Dove

EACH YEAR FOR THE SPRING EQUINOX, all the forest creatures large and small gathered in the clearing near Barbett Woods for the Mystery Celestial Sweepstakes. The dulcet melody of Dove's beautiful song drew all the animals to her. Coyote nestled up against the tree. Rabbit hopped through the long grass. Squirrel scurried out from his burrow by the trading post. Deer trotted over the spring daffodils, taking care not to trample the first blooms of the new season. Even Elk wandered in for the exciting once-a-year event.

As the leader of the Celestial Council, Owl took his position atop the Infinity Star. The animals gathered near the five-pointed marvel for one of the most thrilling and invigorating events to take place in the woods. This celebration was a special time for all the forest creatures. On this day, the Sun was directly above the Equator, thus making day and night nearly equal in length. Light and darkness were balanced.

Owl began by reviewing the rules, as he did every year. There were three. First, each animal was given one, and only one, ticket. Second, winning was to be kept a secret. In Barbett Woods, it was considered dishonorable to tell the other creatures of one's good fortune. And the third rule was that the winning ticket must be redeemed at midnight at Monkey's Market on the far end of the forest where it meets with the Sanguine River.

On each ticket there were eight earthly symbols. The number eight was known to be a very lucky number in Barbett Woods, as it was a symbol of infinity and was said to represent a constant flow of energy. The Earth, the Sun, and the Moon represented life, clarity, and the rhythm of time. Seeds, Wildflowers, Butterflies, and Eggs symbolized hope, potential, transformation, and renewal. Ostara, the Goddess of Spring, embodied new beginnings.

Every symbol displayed on the ticket had to match the one on the Star and be in the same specific order to win. Thus, in all the conceivable ways a row of symbols could be arranged without repetition, over forty thousand permutations were possible. If one was lucky enough to win a prize and not reveal themselves, rich rewards would be provided for all in the coming year.

Prizes were kept a mystery until they were claimed at the market just outside of Barbett Woods, and they were rumored to be more valuable than thousands of Ostara eggs. Ostara eggs were not like regular eggs. These small eggs, made of precious, gem-like stone, were often traded in the woods for goods and services.

Dove was perched right in front of the towering Star. At this hour the Sun peered through the magnificent bur oak. Openings between the far-reaching branches of the nearly one-hundred-foot-wide crown provided just the right amount of light without too much glare or deep shadow.

Most birds have amazing eyesight, but not Dove. She was not well, and her vision was diminishing with each passing year. The Earth's expeditious orbit around the Sun yet again was a stark reminder of how brief life is. Dove had spoken of winning ever since she was a young fledgling.

Owl reached up with his majestic wing and spun the Infinity Star. All the animals looked on with excitement. Rabbit hopped in the air, twisted, and landed back on the ground, all the while twitching his nose and inhaling the sweet aroma springtime brings. Squirrel chattered while nibbling through the shell of an acorn. Deer's tail swished from side to side in anticipation. Raccoon trilled and Elk trumpeted.

The Infinity Star spun, ticking and clacking as it went round and round. The center of the Star was made up of eight concentric circles, each containing eight symbols, and it was designed in such a way that the symbols would not repeat. None of the animals knew quite how it worked, but that was part of the magic. The symbols were just a blur as they went whizzing by. As the Star slowed down, the time between each tick and clack grew. Then the circles came to a halt one by one. From the center outward to the top point of the Star, the winning combination was displayed.

Dove's eyes glowed with a glimmer of light. She'd finally won a prize in the sweepstakes! Almost as if in one continuous motion, Dove joyously lifted her head high and then lowered it in dismay. While keeping the secret was important, traveling outside of the forest was not safe for Dove.

Dove could forfeit the ticket altogether or risk her life to collect the prize. She was running out of options, and it was impossible for her to keep it a secret that she had won. Collecting the prize herself would be a dangerous task.

So she closed her eyes for a moment and prayed, *Ostara, please forgive me for what I am about to do. I know that I might not be honorable, but I shall make it up and share my good fortune with another.* Dove discreetly showed the ticket to her friend Coyote.

Coyote looked over the ticket carefully, but he did not see a winning combination. Coyote knew Dove would be heartbroken to find out she didn't really win. Coyote paused for a brief moment and said, "Yes, you did win. It's true."

Coyote offered to redeem the ticket for Dove because of her fading vision. He knew the nighttime flight was far too dangerous for her. She'd have to avoid larger birds like hawks and eagles. Although the trek might not be the safest for him, Coyote had good night vision and could dodge predators, cover ground quickly, and avoid obstacles.

Dove circled above Coyote's head for a moment, then flew down and nuzzled against his welcoming snout. "Please be careful," Dove said with a raspy coo.

When nightfall arrived, Coyote gathered up all the Ostara eggs he could muster and put them in a bandanna, taking care not to drop any, and then headed to the market. As Coyote made his way out of his den, his peripheral vision alerted him to the large brown bear looming over the moonlit ground below. The forest was rich with the musk of the bear's scent markings. Coyote skulked along the tree line to avoid being noticed. Thanks to his quick thinking, Coyote escaped a potentially deadly encounter with a ferocious bear—or so he thought.

In an instant, he was face-to-face with the rapacious bear. With its massive front legs, the bear was about to crash down on Coyote when he launched himself at the bear's left hind leg, knocking the bear off balance. The bear was startled and confused. Coyote sped off into the night, continuing his journey.

Coyote kept trekking along the treacherous trail. He jumped over logs and dodged low-hanging branches as he traversed the uneven terrain with newfound confidence and bravery.

In his approach to the market, Coyote noticed three hunters. It was not uncommon to see huntsmen near the market, given its close proximity to the Sanguine River. Because of the variety of animals that lived near the river, it was an attractive place for hunters.

Close to finishing his harrowing journey, Coyote vowed not to let it end at the hands of a hunter—or three, for that matter. Coyote let out his most powerful howl with such tremendous force that his gigantic breath propelled the hunters into the air. Seconds later all three woodsmen came crashing to the ground. Coyote darted toward the entrance of the market.

Once he was safely inside, Coyote looked at all of the items for sale. Coyote was a gent of little means, but he knew he had to obtain a prize befitting Dove.

Coyote tossed all the Ostara eggs in his possession onto the counter and asked, "What can I get for these?"

Monkey counted them out. There were a mere eleven Ostara eggs in all. Monkey showed Coyote to the small display case by the door. It contained a small purse with a frayed strap, a mirror that was more fog than reflection, and a pair of mismatched gloves. There was not much to choose from and certainly nothing that looked like it would be a prize befitting the Mystery Celestial Sweepstakes.

Coyote bowed his head. He needed a prize suitable for Dove. As he raised his head again he saw, on the wall behind Monkey, a necklace that sparkled like the twinkling sky on a clear summer night.

"How much for the necklace hanging on the wall?" Coyote asked.

Monkey replied, "Oh, you mean the Celestial Necklace of Light. That is not for sale. That was given to my grandmother by her grandmother."

Coyote pleaded with Monkey. "You see, I fear I have done something with the intention of a good heart but which I cannot oblige."

"What do you mean?" asked Monkey.

"Dove's eyesight is poor, and she thought she won a prize from the sweepstakes celebrating the Spring Equinox earlier today. I led her to believe that she did," Coyote explained.

"Can you keep a secret?" Monkey asked.

"Of course I can. And I most certainly will," Coyote answered.

Monkey began telling Coyote the story behind the Celestial Necklace. "My great-great-grandmother believed that a noble act of selflessness is the greatest gift you can give."

"I do too," Coyote said with a tear in his eye.

Monkey handed over the necklace and said, "Then the necklace is yours for all that you have already given me, because your love for Dove is the most selfless and pure love I have ever seen. Safe travels, and goodnight. "

Coyote left with the necklace and headed home, grateful for Monkey's kind spirit.

* * *

The Sun's first rays bounced off the necklace and created a stunning glow reminiscent of dawn's first light. Coyote visited Dove's nest the next morning and presented her with her good fortune.

"Every dawn brings new beginnings." Coyote read the inscription and, in a delicate gesture, placed the necklace upon Dove.

Dove embraced Coyote and whispered, “Ostara will reward you for your kindness to me.”

“She already has, my beloved Dove,” Coyote responded.

On that day, Ostara’s magic and the spirit of dawn were felt throughout Barbett Woods, a gentle reminder that every day a new opportunity for good arises.

Dana Bree
Entering the Heart of Darkness

IT ALL STARTED AT A GOING-AWAY PARTY in my loft building on lower Broadway in New York. My best friend, Trix, who lives on the fifth floor, invited her closest friends to a bon voyage party she was throwing for herself. She was leaving for a yearlong journey to the Philippines to photograph and document the rebels in the Cordillera Mountains. I was missing her already and didn't know how I was going to handle the big hole in my life when I could no longer pop down to the fifth floor for a cup of coffee or a glass of wine.

The loft was packed, the music blasting out Aretha Franklin's thumping "Freeway of Love" then melting into the Pointer Sisters' "Neutron Dance." I was leaning against the wall, bopping along with the beat, a glass of wine in my hand, watching friends gyrate to the music, when the elevator door opened. Chris and Muriel, from the ninth floor, came in with their own surprise guest. He had pale blond hair, sapphire-blue eyes, and sun-kissed skin. He was lean and wiry-looking and wore a double-breasted navy blazer and gray slacks—a bit formal for this raucous crowd, but not off-putting at all. I stopped dead in my tracks. He was a dead ringer for Peter O'Toole, I thought. I couldn't take my eyes off him.

"Dana, come and meet my cousin, Rex," said Muriel. "He just arrived from Botswana, so I brought him along."

"Nice to meet you, Dana," he said as he held out his hand. His voice was a cross between British aristocrat and South African drawl. I have to say that a person's voice can seduce me every time, and this was no exception. Despite his resemblance to Peter O'Toole, it hardly mattered who he looked like at all; it was the sound of his voice that beguiled me. It's no wonder I was smitten.

Botswana? Who is this person? I thought as I shyly took his hand. As I stared into his eyes, I felt a tremor run through me, like something dangerous and delicious was about to happen.

He winked at me and grinned.

"Is this your first time here?" I asked him. The rest of the room ceased to exist. I was in a cocoon of possibility, and I knew I had never met anyone like him before.

"I've been wanting to visit for a really long time, but I have been working in Chobe Game Lodge in Botswana as head chef and dogs' body and I needed a break," he said.

"What does dogs' body mean?" I asked him. "I've never heard that phrase before."

"It's just something I say. It means that I was always on call to do anything that needed done at the lodge."

The only thing I knew about Botswana was from a wacky movie I saw a couple of years ago called *The Gods Must Be Crazy*, about a Bushman encountering the stranger aspects of modern civilization. Rex might as well have said that he arrived from the moon, as much as I knew about Africa, let alone Botswana.

"Is it a hunting lodge or a photo safari lodge?" I asked him, hoping that it wasn't a place where hunters came and slaughtered wild animals just so they could take them home, mount their heads on den walls, and brag about how brave they were.

"It's paradise. No shooting the animals unless they shoot first. Just kidding," he quickly interjected when he noticed the look of horror on my face. "In fact, poachers can be shot on sight. Botswana takes its animal preservation seriously."

"Good," I said, and I meant it. He called it paradise. I never even considered traveling to Africa. It just seemed to be too complicated and expensive to even figure out where I would start. I had read *Out of Africa* by Karen Blixen and was captivated by the true tales of the author's coffee farm in Kenya, her beloved Kikuyu workers, and her love affair with the bush pilot Denys Finch Hatton. Like Scheherazade and her *One Thousand and One Nights*, Blixen seduced Denys with her storytelling and kept him coming back for more, the same way she enchanted all of us who read her story. But this took place starting in 1914, when Africa was at its colonial peak and less dangerous than I am sure it is today.

I wanted to talk with Rex, not just try to make myself heard over the loud music and laughter of all the people in the room with their drunken, shallow chatter.

As if reading my mind, he looked at me and said, "It's noisy in here. Can we go someplace quiet for a cup of coffee?"

"We should hang out a while longer. It's Trix's party. Let me introduce you."

I introduced him to Trix, who, by the look on her face, took an immediate dislike to him. We had been friends for a long time, and she knew me well enough to recognize that I was going to get to know this guy better. And she wouldn't be around to give me her advice and save me from myself.

We stayed at the party for another hour, then I invited him up to my loft on the seventh floor where I made a pot of coffee. We talked half the night. He told me about Africa, and I told him about New York. We were interested in each others' experiences living on opposite sides of the world. I had been planning another trip to Central America in the spring, but now all I wanted was to experience the African bush and the forests and the animals of Botswana. I also wanted to finish getting my pilot's license, which I had started as a teenager. What better place than Africa?

"Come to Africa. Be a pilot, Chuchi. You can make money; there's a need for pilots. You could really help make a difference," he said as we lay in my bed watching the rising sun's rays gleaming through the floor to ceiling windows onto the oak floors of my expansive loft.

"What does Chuchi mean?" I asked him, curious.

"Chuchi is a pet name, the same as babe or sweetie. Is it all right if I call you that?" he asked.

I smiled and kissed him. "You can call me whatever you like."

I looked at him, visions filling my brain: flying over the African veld, watching the migrations of thousands of wildebeest and the herds of elephants as they trampled everything in their path. But reality set in. I couldn't imagine who would hire an American woman who just got her pilot's license. Still, it was worth fantasizing about. I just knew I wanted a break from the stress and constant rumble of cars and buses on the streets of New York, and the shrill police sirens and firetrucks as they raced down Broadway at all hours of the day and night. The odor of gas and oil and garbage and urine was a reminder that I lived in a major metropolitan city, and I couldn't remember what an unpolluted world was like. I was tired of the deadlines with my job, even though I loved being a designer. I yearned for another kind of adventure.

Is it possible that I could go to Africa and become a Beryl Markham? She wrote the most amazing book that I read the previous year, called *West with the Night*, a memoir of her life as a professional pilot, horse trainer, and adventurer in Africa in the 1940s. And now I had met this man who was opening up a door to a world that I knew nothing about. He told me he needed to go back to take care of some business for a couple of weeks and asked if I would like to come to Africa.

It seemed like a miracle. I had a personal invitation to enter an unknown new world. I did not hesitate. I agreed to step through this magical portal and only worried that it was all an illusion, that it would shimmer like an oasis in the desert and disappear around me, leaving me in the arid sands of my disappointment.

At critical points in my life like this, I always think of my favorite poem by Langston Hughes. It starts out:

What happens to a dream deferred?
Does it dry up like a raisin in the sun?
Or fester like a sore—
And then run? . . .
Or does it explode?

I have always tried to keep my dried-up raisins to a minimum and my explosions from getting me into too much trouble. But as a philosophy for living, it has made my life interesting. And now I was about to move into a whole new realm.

I must admit, I don't know what seduced me first. Was it the handsome Rex with his stories of living and working in Africa, or was I already primed because of my fascination with everything I read about Africa when I was barely a teenager? And as an adult, I thrilled to the stories that Isak Dinesen and Beryl Markham wrote about women taking their place in Africa. Whatever it was, Rex was giving me a personal invitation to enter an unknown new world. I did not hesitate. I said yes.

* * *

Two weeks later — Leaving the known world

Rex had left two days ago. He already had a return ticket so we weren't flying together, but the plan was that he would pick me up at Victoria Falls Airport on the border between Zambia and Zimbabwe, then drive to Chobe Game Lodge at the top of Botswana.

As I was waiting for my flight to begin boarding at JFK, I had no idea what awaited me. But each time I said these African names out loud, I felt like I was on a journey back in time: Botswana, Zambia, Swaziland, South Africa, Zimbabwe. I remembered reading books about the Boer War, and the Zulus, one of the fiercest African tribes that ever existed. What adventures are to be had on the continent portrayed in *Heart of Darkness*, even during these modern times? I could not begin to imagine the experiences this trip would offer me or just how removed I would become from everything I was familiar with.

After I arrived at Gatwick International Airport, I reboarded onto Zambian Airways. Sixteen hours later I awoke. It was four a.m. I couldn't sleep any more. Through the porthole window, the stars shone like glitter strewn across the black velvet gown of the sky. A sudden streak of light shot across my view out the window. A comet, a dying star? A premonition of things to come?

* * *

The rumble of the plane's engines changed, the overhead lights came on, and I smelled coffee brewing. As I looked through the tiny window, I glimpsed what I thought was the shimmer of a silvery lake. As the plane descended, the lake I had perceived turned out to be the top layer of clouds, the edge of the world. Dropping lower, we entered that amorphous netherworld of white where it felt like up and down didn't really exist, just a through-the-rabbit-hole timeless moment. My ears popped. The mist lifted and, through a break in the clouds, I saw a river far below, a thin, sinuous line of molten gold. My pulse quickened.

* * *

Lusaka Airport, Zambia

As I disembarked from the plane and started down the stairs, I was enveloped in hot, humid air, and sweat bubbled from every pore. Lots of dark-skinned, fierce-looking men in military uniforms were standing around, hugging their old Kalashnikov, assault rifles and directing the passengers to the main terminal. It looked like a huge rusting Quonset hut, surrounded by piles of trash and a dark, mysterious jungle beyond. But the light was golden, and the foreignness was quite unlike any place I had ever been before. Despite the heat and the guns and the overheated jungle greenery, I found the otherworldliness of it mesmerizing and a bit frightening at the same time.

After I walked the through the open doors of the terminal, I looked around for the transit lounge, or what passed for one. I had six hours to wait for my next flight to take me on to Victoria Falls. The soldiers inside the terminal directed all the passengers into a single line where they questioned each person about their health card. I had no health card with me. Who said anything about a health card? I thought. Finally, I was standing in front of a guard who looked at me and demanded my health card.

"I am not staying in Zambia, not even leaving the airport, just traveling through," I insisted.

"But madam, you must have a health card or get injections," he insisted right back. There was no arguing with a guy with a gun who had received orders to make sure everyone had a health card. There wasn't even a spark of humor in his dark eyes.

I looked over at the line of people queuing up for their injections to get the required health card. *Yikes. This is really bad. The nurse is using the same needle on everyone.* The first thing I could think of came out of my mouth. "I have to use the ladies' room first." I hurriedly removed myself to a foul-smelling bathroom and waited for everyone to clear out. An hour later, the line of people was gone, the soldiers no longer herding everyone through the health card station. Whew! The coast was clear, so I collected my luggage and walked over to the transit lounge. Six hours later I boarded my flight for Harare by way of Victoria Falls, without a health card.

Victoria Falls

The flight over Victoria Falls was spectacular. Before this, I had only seen pictures in books of this magnificent force of nature. According to a pamphlet in my seat pocket, experts consider it the world's largest waterfall based on its width and height combined. It was said to be almost double the height of Niagara Falls. In the Bantu language it is called Mosi-oa-Tunya, or The Smoke That Thunders. In the Tonga language it is Shungu Namutitima, or Boiling Water. There's also an older name, Chongwe, which means The Place of the Rainbow, but none of these names do it justice. Even over the rumble of the plane's engines hundreds of feet in the air as we got ready to land, I heard the roar of the water.

After circling over the falls, the plane landed at Livingstone Airport on the northern edge of Livingstone, Zambia. I got off, despite my official itinerary. It had me flying on to Harare, Zimbabwe, and staying over for two days. Then I would board another plane back again to this same airport just forty kilometers from my final destination, the Zimbabwe border post right across the bridge from Zambia. The airline schedules here were insane and made little sense. I trusted Rex had the same idea that I did in ignoring the schedule and just doing what made sense. I hoped it wasn't my first mistake.

After disembarking, I gathered my luggage and took a shuttle bus forty kilometers to the Zambian border post. I filled out my personal identification papers and visa requests and got my passport stamped, all of which were necessary to walk across the Victoria Falls Bridge and enter Zimbabwe. It was a hot and sunny day, humid from the steam of the falls filling the air. It took me about fifteen minutes to walk from the border post to the bridge, hauling my suitcase on little plastic wheels. Halfway across the bridge, I stopped and gazed at one of the most famous sights in the world. My heart thrilled with the power of millions of tons of water crashing over the cliff and down, down, down to the cauldron far below. It was so far down that all I could see was mist, and it looked like smoke curling up through the air until it reached high into the sky. The force of it mesmerized me for I don't know how long. I turned at last and finished crossing the bridge, then walked another fifteen minutes to the Zimbabwe border post where, with fingers crossed, I hoped to meet Rex.

Once again, I entered a border post, filled out my identification papers and visa request, and got my passport stamped. I stepped outside and settled down on the bench in front of the building to wait. I found a working phone at the post and tried calling to leave a message for Rex at Chobe Game Lodge, where he had worked for the past six years. Phones there were not the best, but finally I made a very scratchy connection and left a message. But, as I was to learn, leaving a message was like floating a balloon into the air. You never knew where it would land or who would receive it, if anyone at all.

After an hour and a half and no Rex, I started getting nervous. What if he decided to pick me up on the Zambia side? Anything was possible, and I was alone in a strange world with no one to contact. So I grabbed my suitcase and started back across the bridge to return to the Zambian border post. Half an hour later I was back at the post, and I explained my situation to the border guards. They were pleasant but absolutely steadfast. Since I had returned to their country, I had to fill out the paperwork all over again—everything. Once done, I sat and waited for another hour, but I was getting edgier by the minute. What was there to do but go back across the bridge again?

I probably hold the record for the greatest number of times someone has walked back and forth across the Victoria Falls Bridge in one day hauling a suitcase. Six times I made the trek, and six times I filled out identification papers and visa requests and got my passport stamped. The border guards greeted me cheerfully each time but never once budged an inch on proper border-crossing procedure.

It was late in the afternoon. I was exhausted and starting to freak because I didn't know what I was going to do if Rex didn't show up. I decided that I would try to find a ride back to Livingstone, Zambia, and find a place to stay. That's when a dusty Land Rover roared into the parking area—and out stepped Rex. He looked annoyed, probably thinking he had lost his American before she even arrived. "Chuchi, why didn't you stick to the schedule? I got your message this morning and had to drive 108 miles."

"Seriously? The original schedule was crazy. It had me flying to Harare, waiting two days, then getting on another plane and coming back almost to the same place I am now. That made little sense at all. I knew you would figure it out," I said with a smile.

He didn't even ask how my trip was, whether I was OK, or about anything else that might have happened to me. And he was worried about driving 108 miles? How much did I really know about this man? Spending time in New York was one thing, but traversing the pitfalls of Africa was a whole different experience. I took a deep breath. I was here; he was here; I was safe—for now.

He grabbed my suitcase and tossed it into the back of the vehicle.

"We have to go right now. If we don't make the border crossing before sunset the road will be closed."

"Really, they close the road at sunset? Why would they do that?"

"Because they collect a toll, and the men working the border post want to be home before the sun sets. It's too dangerous for them to be walking after dark." That gave me something to think about. What terrors await in the dark?

As he fishtailed out of the border post, I tried to calm myself and be grateful that he had arrived at last to pick me up. My heart finally stopped racing as I watched the scenery flashing by. It was almost too noisy to talk in the Land Rover, but I asked questions about what I was seeing. The most arresting sight was the giant baobab trees. They are curious-looking trees with leaves on top that resemble an umbrella sitting on top of a tall, thick barrel of a trunk.

"Do these trees store water in their trunks?" I asked Rex.

"That's a bit of a myth. They use any water stored for the new leaves. I haven't heard of anyone tapping it to get drinking water. A good question, though," Rex answered.

Away from the falls, the landscape was dry and wide open. The road was dirt, and only one other vehicle traveled in the opposite direction. But there were African children herding goats, a woman with a large jar on her head, and a man riding a rickety bicycle. It was much more primitive than I had imagined.

After driving more than an hour, we hit a stretch of blacktop. Even in the Land Rover, I felt the heat radiating up from the road and warming my arm, which hung out the window. I was leaning back and drowsing when I felt a sharp bump under the tire. I looked behind us and was stunned to see a long ribbon of iridescent green whirling in the air. The afternoon sun's golden rays reflected off its glistening body, and it seemed to stay suspended in the air much longer than I thought could be possible.

"Green mamba," Rex said when he noticed what I was staring at. "She was warming herself on the highway and I didn't notice her. We are really lucky. Those snakes are incredibly fast, and she could just as easily have flipped herself into the back of the vehicle."

I was left shaken by the nearness of the danger but astonished at her beauty. "Did we kill her?" I asked, hoping that we didn't take the life of such a gorgeous creature.

"I don't think so," he said. "They are quite resilient and can withstand all kinds of injuries. She will crawl off into the bush and coil up in a leafy tree branch for a couple of days until she is able to move off again."

"So, why do you call her a her? Are green mambas female?"

"No, but I just do it naturally because the black mambas are so much deadlier. They can outrun a man once they decide to go after you, and their bite is lethal."

I didn't even want to think of such a thing happening. That was not the way I wanted to leave this world.

It was just about sundown when we pulled up at the toll booth. It wasn't really a booth at all but a barrel on each side of the road with a fallen tree trunk across it. A couple of guys wearing backpacks stepped in front, waving us down.

"You must turn around. The road is closed. Come back tomorrow."

Rex, using his most laid-back and respectful tone of voice, said, "But gentlemen, you are still here, and we are here, and we have to get through tonight."

"No, you may not go. It is closed. That is final."

"But maybe I can give you something special if you would do me a favor, just this once."

I watched Rex expertly manipulate these guys into giving him what he wanted. There was no question that we would get through. It was about finding the right price and showing respect.

The two toll takers looked at each other and grinned. They straightened up a bit and looked toward the back of the Land Rover as if they were used to such requests and wanted to see if there was anything interesting in the vehicle. Rex got out and handed each one a blanket and a cheap bottle of whiskey. "Do you think you could do us a favor and just open up the gate this one time?" he asked again.

"Just this once." The older fellow nodded and waved us through.

After we drove through the open gate, I asked, "Do you bribe the locals all the time?"

"This is Africa; there is always a way to get what you want if you come prepared," Rex said.

The sun's last rays of the day blanketed the road and the gently rolling hills in a soft orange glow. Then the first stars of the evening blinked into existence like candles being lit in a dark room. It looked like a fairy-tale painting.

The luxury of the smooth, paved road lasted a short couple of miles. From then on, it was a slow, bumpy ride over potholes and deep ruts.

"Even if we could go faster, it wouldn't be a good idea," Rex said. "The last thing you want to do is hit an elephant. Their mud-covered hides don't reflect the headlights. We could be on top of them before we even had a chance to step on the brakes; too late to stop, and you do not want to see an angry elephant coming for you in the dark."

"Whoa. Do you mean there are elephants all around us?" My first thought was a real Dorothyism: I am not in Kansas anymore.

"Better safe than sorry," he said. "For both us and the elephant."

Despite looking for elephants in the dark, I wasn't in a hurry. The air was soft and warm; the sky was a rich, velvety black filled with the brightest stars I had ever seen. There was no electric light contamination, and the air was pollution-free—some of the benefits of pre-industrialization. Occasionally we would pass a campfire a couple of hundred yards into the bush and see the dark silhouettes of people gathered around laughing and eating. I could smell meat cooking on a spit and the sound of singing and drumming. But I did not see any electric lights, nor hear any machines or engines other than the rattle and rumble of our Land Rover.

* * *

Half dozing, I was awakened by the clicking of the engine when the vehicle stopped.

"We are here, Chuchi," Rex announced. He sounded tired, as I am sure he was after driving for hours to collect me from Victoria Falls and then driving back in the dark.

It was hard to see where "here" really was, but the first thing I noticed was the faint grumble of a generator and the soft glow of low-key electric lighting illuminating the path to the entrance. A young African man, dressed in a crisp khaki shirt and shorts, rushed out and greeted us effusively.

"Mr. Rex, welcome back. I hope you had a pleasant trip." The young man was slim as a cattail and had the whitest teeth I had ever seen. He had smooth, dark skin and beautiful, cinnamon-brown eyes.

"Hello, Motswane. This is my friend Dana," Rex said.

I reached out to shake his hand. At first, he hesitated, but then he shyly touched my hand and shook gently, a big smile gracing his face.

From my guidebook I had read on the plane, Botswana is a rich culture, and the predominant ethnic group is the Tswana, which makes up over 80 percent of the population. When combined with the other 20 percent of different ethnic groups, they are collectively called "Batswana," meaning people of Botswana. They name their children names that relate to great deeds, aspirations, God, and success and family businesses. Motswane is a simple, pure name which translates to "good." At first glance it seemed an appropriate name.

Motswane led the way through the front doors of one of the most beautiful buildings I had ever seen. The door lintels were hand-carved mahogany tree trunks polished to a deep luster. The floor was slate tile in grays and blues and rust hues, and there were African tapestries and paintings on the walls. Brass sconces lined the walls, the gold light creating the perfect ambiance for late in the evening.

We were both hungry, so Rex settled me in a chair on the outdoor dining patio overlooking the Chobe River and headed off to the kitchen to fix us something simple. He was the head chef at Chobe Game Lodge and had been for the past six years. When the lodge was being rebuilt in the early '80s, they hired Rex to move to the bush and help with the reconstruction and then take over as head chef when the lodge reopened. The original owners built it in 1972 and created the first five-star safari lodge in Botswana; it was the only lodge ever allowed inside Chobe National Park.

I heard the coo of night doves and what sounded like a deep honking laugh. I had no idea what that was, but it seemed to come from the river.

I walked over to the railing and stared down at the water, trying to see what was making the noise. There were large, dark floating masses that would splash and then disappear.

Rex returned with a tray holding two plates of food and a couple glasses of wine and set it down on the table. I went back and sat down. "Thank you for finding me, Rex. I wasn't sure if my message would get through."

He looked at me, took my hand, and kissed my fingers. "Everyone knows me in this part of the world. All you have to do is mention my name."

I looked at him and nodded, then started eating. The food was delicious: roast chicken, green beans, and fresh bread. And the white wine was ice cold.

The strange coughing, laughing noise started up again. "Rex, what is that sound? It sounds like someone laughing, but really strangely."

"Hippos, Chuchi; hippos enjoying an evening floating in the river. They make that sound when they are happy or just chatting with their mates. Hippos are very social with each other, but not so much with people. They are very aggressive if anyone gets in their way. Hippos kill more people than any other animal in Africa."

"Whoa! That's not funny. The only hippos I know anything about are the kind wearing pink tutus in a Walt Disney cartoon."

We finished the late evening meal, drank the wine, and headed off to our room. Since Rex worked here, we had access to one of the executive suites with a balcony overlooking the river and a small private swimming pool. Everything was luxurious, including a modern bathroom. The white towels were thick and soft. The ceiling fan circled lazily above the bed, which was encased in a white mosquito net. It was like a painting from the Victorian era. After a quick shower, we turned out the lights and climbed into bed. Our lovemaking was gentle, both of us exhausted from the day's events.

Even as tired as I was, it still took me a long time to go to sleep. There were so many night noises: squeals and rumblings, howls and growls, and hippos laughing at their own personal jokes.

Tomorrow would be another day in the heart of Africa, and I did not know what awaited me, but I had started my journey.

Elaine Leet
Gus and Martha

MOST DAYS OLD GUS WISHED HE COULD SEE his wife's face again, her smile, her unruly hair, her eyes that changed from blue to gray with her mood. For nearly a decade Gus yearned to hear his wife's laughter and her curt comebacks to his stories. Not today. He knew her eyes would be firing up today. Martha wasn't going to be best pleased with his news. No, today it was just as well that he could not see her face or hear her reactions.

Gus stood alone in the cemetery high on a Virginia mountain, watching the sun sink into the Appalachians. His time was running out. His eyes watered, only partially protected from the weather by the brim of his red and black wool hunter's cap. He blamed his tears on the biting November wind whistling over the ridge, but he knew he wasn't being honest in that.

At her ethereal workbench next to her headstone, Martha looked up from drawing an outline on a block of wood and grunted, "Here he comes, and high time. Probably been down to Harry's Diner. Probably a new waitress to flirt with."

"Good afternoon, Martha, my dear. I'm late. I apologize. Better late than never."

"Humph. Better never late, Gus." Martha's tongue stuck out just a bit as she concentrated on getting the sketched line just right.

"November's not messing around this year. Winter's on us. The wind has got to be twenty degrees colder and a sight stronger up here in the cemetery. Still got a few leaves hanging on down in the valley. Your asters are going to seed. I brought you the last of the blossoms. I'll just tuck them up close to your headstone so the wind can't blow them away."

Martha nodded, noting, "Those purple ones were always the last to go. I don't suppose you gathered up some of the seeds for next spring." She held the block of wood at arms' length and rotated it to inspect all sides.

"I was down to Harry's this morning and heard a joke I think you'll like, Martha. Now be patient while I zip up this new coat. Damn arthritis has my knuckles all swollen. Makes everything harder. Got a good deal on it at the Army surplus yesterday. See, Martha, it's got all these pockets with zippers and snaps. I can carry anything I might need. Just can't remember which pocket it's in. That boy Carl, you know, Mickey's son? He gave me a real good deal."

Martha looked up and sniffed. "I see you've forgotten everything I tried to teach you about buying clothes, that's what I see. That coat probably was a bargain. Who else would buy it? It's got no style and it's too big. I always liked that peacoat you wore when we were dating. It brought out the blue in your eyes. Mind you don't catch that overgrown goatee in the zipper. Wouldn't want you to lose what little you've got left of that gray hair."

"Cold weather bothers me more this fall, Martha. Chills me right to the bone." Gus tried again to align the pin with the slider and box. "Damn," he whispered, missing the mark again. "Ah, now I got it." Gus pulled the zipper tab to his throat with a shiver. "I miss that ham soup you used to make. That started warming me through to my bones as soon as I opened the front door and caught a whiff. I can still conjure up that bacony, oniony smell."

Martha smiled, turning the wood to sketch on another face of the cube. "Get on with the joke, you old goat."

"All right. Now listen. And don't interrupt, or I'll forget the punch line."

Martha shook her head as she used her chisel to carve the outline on the first face of the cube.

Gus adjusted his hat's earflaps and tugged his gloves over his swollen arthritic fingers.

Martha looked up. "Look at you, your eyes sparkling and you grinning like you're Bob Hope or that late night comedian with the English accent. When they smile like that you know there's a good bit coming. Well, get on with it, old man."

Never one to be hurried, Gus continued in his soft-spoken way as he had all his life:

There's a busy road, like the old sawmill road after the state black-topped it. On one side is a beautiful green field with a large pond. On the other side is a field of dry hay stubble with a large mud puddle and three geese. These geese are late to fledge, and they still can't fly. The first goose's named Foot. The second goose's named Foot Foot, and the third goose's named Foot Foot Foot.

Martha observed dryly, "Not much for naming in that family." She switched to a knife to add detail to her carving.

Gus continued.

One day Foot tells his brothers, "Foot Foot and Foot Foot Foot, I'm going to cross this road to get to the nice green field and that lovely pond."

Foot Foot shakes his feathers and protests, "Foot, don't do it. You'll get run over."

Foot says, "I don't care, Foot Foot. I'm sick of this horrible dried-up place."

Foot walks over to the road while Foot Foot and Foot Foot Foot watch. Foot starts waddling across the road, dodging cars. There's a lot of honking, and the cars make a lot of noise too. Brakes squeal. To Foot Foot and Foot Foot Foot's astonishment, Foot makes it across.

Foot glances back, stretches to his full height, and announces with a strut, "I've made it, Foot Foot and Foot Foot Foot!"

Foot Foot and Foot Foot Foot sigh in relief and make a pact to never cross the road.

A few days later, Foot Foot Foot wonders to Foot Foot, "How do you think Foot is getting on?"

"Let's go see," his brother suggests.

Foot Foot and Foot Foot Foot walk to the road and discover Foot's lifeless body in the ditch. They decide to risk their lives to drag Foot back to their side of the highway and bury him. Foot Foot Foot digs the hole and Foot Foot lowers Foot into it and says, in the way of brothers, "We told him not to go. Dumb little drake." Then he adds some nice words, and the ceremony is complete.

A few more days pass and Foot Foot Foot says, "Foot Foot, I'm going to cross this road to get to that fine looking pond."

Foot Foot says, "Are you kidding, Foot Foot Foot? We've already got one Foot in the grave!"

Martha rested her knife on the table and laughed. "You always could spin a yarn and set the girls to giggling. I was no exception." She picked up the chisel and started on the second face of the block.

"I remember, Martha, that a joke would always get me forgiven when I made a blunder like being late today. So, do you forgive me?"

Martha chuckled and shrugged her shoulders. "So cute even with the crow's feet and the lines you try to hide with your dreadful beard. Forgiven. Move on." She started smoothing the edges of the carving.

"You know, Martha, sometimes I can almost hear you talking and almost see you working away at some wood carving project or other. I don't tell anybody else that. They'd call it 'old timers disease' or some such thing and lock me away."

"You're smarter than you look, Gus." Martha flipped the wood over to the third face of the cube.

"I was going through picture albums last night, Martha. You at our eighth-grade graduation with long dark hair to your waist. You as Homecoming Queen with that little crown twinkling in your long blond hair all piled up high on your head, and you giving that Homecoming King a 'keep your hands to yourself' glare. You in that fine white wedding gown with your reddish hair pulled back with a long braid framing your face. You with your salt and pepper hair cut right up short for our last anniversary together. In each one it was your eyes that stood out. Your kaleidoscope eyes, telling me in gray that I was in for an argument or in crystal blue that everything was okay. And, oh, those turquoise eyes that said it was going to be a great night. Do you know, I don't think of you the way you looked at different times of our fifty years together? Just figured that out last night. When I think of you it's sort of overlaid pictures all combined into one. I remember all of you."

"Wow, Gus," Martha said in surprise. "That's a speech. Didn't know you had it in you. Didn't know you saw so much." She carved the outline on the fourth face of the cube.

"Martha, I'm feeling kind of tired, so I'm just gonna lean up against your headstone here and rest my eyes for a minute."

He was quiet for a moment, and Martha laid the wood down to examine the sharp edge of her blade.

Gus cleared his throat. "I remember how it was to be with you. Even on my sixtieth birthday you made me feel young and strong. You remember when I asked you to marry me? I hooked a stray lock of your golden hair back behind your pretty little ear. Traced along your jaw to your chin. You raised your eyes up. Your sweet lips parted. I could feel your breath on my cheek, and the scent of you made my head spin. I tilted your chin to bring your lips nearer my own. I let my lips just touch yours, teasing. Your mouth closed over mine. I pulled you all soft and warm right up close. We just kinda melted into each other. Sweet memories."

Martha's hands stilled. "Mmmm. Sweet memories."

Gus raised his eyes to the sky. "Those clouds look like the ones we saw the day of our wedding. Flying galleons, you called them."

Martha raised her eyes. "I remember."

A tear slipped down the man's weathered cheek. "Martha, I miss you."

The spirit sighed. "I miss you too."

After a time, the old man opened his eyes, but he could not face the grave. Instead, he stared at his feet. Gus dug the toe of his shoe into the dried grass and dirt. "I got some news today. The cancer's back. Doc says my heart won't hold up to another round of chemo. I expect the geese ain't the only ones with one foot in the grave."

Martha's hands faltered and the knife slipped from her fingers. Wood shavings scattered off the edge of the workbench. Shock and joy flashed in waves over her face. "Oh, Gus! Even from here I can't bear the thought of you dying. It's a tough row to hoe, and yet part of me is thrilled that we can really be together again." Her eyes narrowed. "Wait, you're holding something back. What's the rest of the story?"

Gus took a swipe at the tear. "I was up in the middle of the night, back at the full moon, listening to the TV tell how one drug could save you from one ailment while it killed you with another. I looked out the window. Frost gleamed all over everything. Not much to hold me to this life. Then I realized what was important and decided there's only one thing I need to get done before I join you. I thought about it a whole lot. I've got to find a good home for Sally. I know. I know. Sally ain't your favorite subject. You were always jealous, but I swear I loved you more than her, most of the time anyway. She needs looking after and protecting. Those eco-warriors are doing for Sally's kind what Stephen King did for clowns. It's intolerable. It's downright disrespectful of all '69 Mustangs—Sally included."

"Sally? You mean you're staying alive to take care of a car?" Martha scowled. She added fine lines to the fourth face.

"She ain't just a car," Gus said, shaking his head. "Sally's a 1969 Royal Maroon Boss 429 Mustang with a rear sway bar, crescent combustion chamber, and manual hood scoop. She's still got her NASCAR number.

Born to fly, she was." Gus gave the headstone a pleading look. "Remember, Martha, when we flew with Sally? Remember the day Harry challenged us at the light on Main Street and we outran him along the ridge clear to the county line? Dust all over his sad Barracuda." Gus gazed at the headstone. "And you always did appreciate her leather seats." Tones of hopeful apology lingered in his words.

"I did like the leather seats," Martha admitted, "and the smooth ride, and being able to leave that ornery Harry Drinker in the dust at the traffic light. And that ridge ride was a thrill no rollercoaster could match." She scooped into the center of the block and removed wood in slender slices.

"Martha, I got an offer to buy Sally a couple weeks back. Over $100,000. Almost took it. Went and saw the guy. He had cash in hand. Then I figured out he was going to use our Sally for parts. Told me to think of it like being an organ donor." Gus closed his fists as far as the arthritis would permit. He spit the word through gritted teeth: "Barbarian."

Martha tightened her lips. "You did right, Gus, bringing the car back home. Sentiment aside, cutting it up seems cannibalistic." She gouged out a large piece of wood from the center of the block.

"So, there was a Mustang rally in Richmond last Saturday. That new waitress, Bonnie's her name—"

"I knew there was a new waitress in there somewhere." Martha tilted the block to set her blade at exactly the right angle to continue her work.

"—showed me on her phone. Well, one thing led to another, and the upshot was there was a collector gonna be at the rally. He offered $300,000 for Sally, if she passed his inspection."

Martha was indignant. "You're telling me you drove to Richmond? You fool! It's one thing to drive these two-lanes you've known since they were dirt." Martha paused, contemplating the offer. "But $300,000! That's an awful lot of money, Gus. Still, you can't bring it with you." She switched to her smallest blade to begin the detailed work on the center of the carving.

"Now quit your fussing, Martha. I took a couple days and drove the back roads. Took Harry with me. See, it was important. It wasn't just the money. We were ambassadors, so to speak. All along the way we reached out to the poor ignorant voters that think they have to put every internal combustion engine into the smelter to save the planet."

"Oh, yeah, I'm sure you got far with that attitude," Martha snorted. Her hand wielded the blade in quick, precise, minuscule cuts.

"Then we gave 'em a gander at Sally and let 'em take pictures. Gave some rides and next thing you know they were backing our plan for one day a month for vintage vehicles."

"Lucky you weren't shot," Martha observed.

"So, Martha, we headed on to Richmond and found out the rally was up at Doswell. Well, we stopped at a mom-and-pop outside a little bitty town called—now I'll spell it for you—B-u-m-p-a-s-s. And we were sipping our coffee and discussing whether or not the mom-and-pop folks would take offense if we asked if their neck of the woods was called bum-pass or bump-ass. And next thing we know there's all these Mustangs pulled into the parking lot. Drivers were all sorts. All ages. And they said they heard what we were doing, and they wanted us to join up with their caravan and lead a kind of parade around the governor's mansion. So we followed them through the city to this long driveway. Then we took the lead so as Sally would be right up front. It's a real long driveway, Martha. All around there's those orange and yellow fall flowers and such. You'd like it, I think. There was a crew setting up Christmas lights, but they didn't bother us.

"Then Sally swung into a loop right at the front door, and if that governor and first lady didn't both come out and get their picture taken. And then, Martha, I ain't kiddin', that man asked if he could drive Sally! Well, Harry climbed into the back, and I took your seat, and that yuppie no-good politician got behind the wheel. I didn't like it, not one bit, Martha, but I sucked it up, being as it was for Sally's future."

The block tilted again as Martha scratched in details. "You chatting with the governor? I'm surprised the commonwealth still stands."

"That lying lawyer drove us right up to his big garage and invited us in to see his 'antique cars,' as he called them. Wasn't much, Martha, just a couple of Ferraris, GTOs, a Porsche, and an Aston Martin. You wouldn't have liked them. Me and Harry caught each other's eye while the bureaucrat was talking, and we smiled along and said nice things. By the time we got back to the big house, news reporters had gathered, and the governor made a speech. We answered some questions. I let Harry talk some about his old 'cuda, but when he wandered into Mustang territory, I did the talking."

"What a surprise," Martha muttered, smoothing the edges and turning the sculpted block to inspect her work, adding a final stroke here and there.

"We didn't have any intention of being leaders, but these folks started following us to Doswell and there we were. Now don't fret, Martha; we stayed off that moving death trap they call I-95. Took US 1. Pretty country once you get out of the shadow of those tall buildings."

"Got to admire you, Gus. After only seventy-six years your 'tribe' finally found you." Martha peered into the center of the carving.

"Martha, along the concourse entering the state fairgrounds—it turns out it's not just for the state fair—anyway, all along the roadway were protestors. They were singin' songs, and carryin' signs, and wearin' gas masks. Some were singing 'Blowin' in the Wind' like we did in the '60s. Some chanted about pulling gas engines and replacing them with electric. They called it conversion engine therapy. I was pretty sure that was made illegal, but Harry said that was a different kind of conversion. One young guy tried to convince me to let him put an electric engine in Sally. He made tearing her guts out sound real gentle and right and—what's that word you used?—benign, that's it. I sent him packing."

Martha frowned. "Well, I should think so!" She set the finished project on her work bench.

"Anyway, there were all these people buying us dinners, and we could have had any drink we wanted, but I was a mite cautious, thinking if I didn't stay sober somebody might make off with Sally. They didn't have any decent 'shine, anyway. Then that collector showed up. We took Sally for his test drive and his mechanic gave her a once-over. Gotta say,

Martha, it took a lot of willpower to put up with him poking around under Sally's hood." Gus drew in a deep breath and shook his head. "Not near so hard as saying goodbye to her though. I just couldn't bring myself to do that. So, I didn't. Sally's down at the house. She's all gassed up and ready to go. I'm just gonna drive and drive. I sorely wish you could take this ride with me, Martha."

She turned the carving in her hands, gazing tenderly at the faces of the man she loved. The first carving was young and smooth with an easy grin. The second carving featured an adult man with a beard, his hair pulled back into a ponytail. The third face had wide sideburns almost to the jaw, and the fourth face had crow's feet and laugh lines at the mouth above a scrawny beard. On each face the eyes caught the light, creating a twinkle. At the center of the carving rose the distinct lines of a Boss 429 Mustang.

"If you think I'm going to just sit here whittling while you go joyriding, you are quite mistaken. Where there's a will there's a way, and I will be right there feeling the wind in my hair as we cruise the ridge."

Gus gave the headstone a pat and made his way out of the cemetery and on down the mountain path toward home. In the driveway, Gus glanced back up the mountain. He ran his hand over Sally's sleek fender and took his seat behind the wheel. When the engine roared, he heard a chuckle from the empty passenger seat.

Gus smiled. "So you found a way, Martha. I hoped you might. No barrier could stand against you once you made your mind up." He tilted the rearview mirror so he could see the passenger seat and grinned at the reflection of Martha sitting in her place.

"Well, what are you waiting for?" Martha ordered, "Let's go!"

Marylou Webster Ambrose
Kindred Spirits

THE FEARSOME THREESOME WERE ENJOYING an afternoon snack in Lois's room when the ghost materialized in front of the flat-screen TV. At first, none of us noticed her. I was taking a cat nap on Lois's lap, and the humans were focused on their chips and cookies. They never paid attention to the TV anyway. If the assisted living aide turned it on after lunch, Lois always turned it off so they could talk.

I startled awake when I sensed electricity in the air. One look at the white figure in front of the TV and my hackles rose. I leaped from lap to windowsill, arching my back and letting out a yowl. Lois glanced up, and the cookie fell out of her open mouth and onto the floor.

Arthur didn't see anything amiss because he's blind, and Rose didn't notice anything because she's almost deaf. Besides, her glasses were so smeared with grease from the potato chips she was eating, she was practically blind too.

"Yikes!" Lois shouted. "Whaaa . . . who . . . ?" She pointed a shaky finger in the direction of the TV.

"What's going on?" half-blind Rose intoned, digging in the bag for more chips.

Arthur sniffed the air, his eyes closed. "Something . . . What is it, Lois?"

Lois gripped the arms of her chair. "I . . . I . . ." she stammered.

"What a sorry bunch," the white-clad figure said, rolling her eyes. "Allow me to introduce myself. I'm Olivia, and I haunt this place."

* * *

Since then, the three humans had been going over and over what happened, trying to make sense of it. Olivia the Ghost had only stayed a few minutes before leaving in a swirl of fog. She promised to return the next day during snack time, depending on her schedule. Cats don't have schedules, so I planned to be there.

"Schedule? What kind of schedule does a ghost have?" Lois asked the others, talking at full volume so Rose could hear.

"Who knows?" Arthur said, just as loud. "Maybe she has other places to haunt."

Rose was silent for a moment. Then she blurted, "I don't believe in ghosts," with a wave of her hand. I happen to know Rose doesn't even believe in outer space.

"But we saw one yesterday," Arthur reminded her. "At least you two did. But I definitely heard her and felt her."

Me too, I thought, from my perch on Lois's lap. Then I went back to licking my paw—in this case, the feline equivalent of biting my nails.

Yesterday Olivia had just started to explain her appearance when footsteps sounded in the hall. "See you tomorrow," she said before making a foggy exit through the heating vent in the ceiling. I observed everything from the relative safety of the windowsill. But if my eyes had gotten any bigger, they'd have fallen out of their sockets and onto the floor.

The Threesome sat stunned, silent, and breathless when Yolanda, the aide, entered the room to gather up the snack leftovers.

"So how are we today?" she asked, dumping empty wrappers and plastic cups in a trash bag. No one answered, but Yolanda never had time to chat anyway, with fifteen other residents to care for. Bag in hand, she hurried out of the room without giving any of us a second look.

Today, Lois, Arthur, and Rose were sitting in their usual places in Lois's room, in front of the turned-off TV. I was purring on Lois's lap, feigning nonchalance. A casual observer wouldn't have noticed anything out of the ordinary. But when Arthur said he felt like he'd just entered the Twilight Zone, the other two agreed. So did I—Lois and I love that old show. Magic was in the air, along with room deodorizer and tonight's fish dinner.

Rose was the only one eating her snack. The rest of us were too nervous.

"Do you think we imagined it?" Lois asked, squeezing her napkin into a ball and pulverizing her cookie inside it. Then she dropped the mess into the wastebasket with a clunk. I watched the cookie's trajectory and decided to fish it out later, after things calmed down.

"No, there was something here, unless you two were playing a practical joke on me," Arthur said with a humph. "Just kidding." Arthur seemed resigned to being blind, but I figured this was one of those times he really wished he could see.

Lois turned to Rose. "What do you think?"

"About what?" Rose said in a monotone, excavating her bag of chips. I knew she didn't like to be bothered when she was eating. Neither did I.

Before Lois could reply, someone gave a loud, barking cough. Our four heads turned, and three of us saw a curl of smoke emerge from under the bed and shape itself into Olivia.

"Don't they ever clean this place?" she complained, picking a dust bunny off her tongue and flicking it away.

Lois's hand flew to her mouth; Arthur turned his head from side to side and said, "Is it her? Is it her?" I flew off Lois's lap and shot into the bathroom.

"Jesus, Mary, and Joseph," Rose said, a chip halfway to her mouth. "Where in hell did you come from?"

Olivia glided in front of the TV and stood facing the little group. She brushed dust off the front of her gauzy white gown, then clasped her hands at her waist. "I guess I owe you all an explanation." She glanced toward the open door. "Could we have some privacy?"

"Privacy?" Lois croaked.

"Yes, so we won't be interrupted like yesterday," Olivia explained. "Lock the door."

Arthur turned toward the sound of Olivia's voice. "We don't have locks in assisted living."

Olivia's brow furrowed. "Is that what this is? A place that helps you live?"

"I call it 'ass living,'" Rose muttered. I'd heard her daughter warn her not to say that, but hell, it always got a laugh.

Olivia chuckled. "You're a feisty one, aren't you? Well, we'll have to make do." She drifted to the door, closed it, and then shoved the desk chair under the knob. "That should buy us some time. Now, allow me to introduce myself properly."

"Rose is hard of hearing, so could you please speak up?" Lois asked. I'm pretty sure Rose's hearing is selective at times.

Taking her place back in front of the TV, Olivia said, "Of course, and I can see you have an impairment as well," she nodded toward Arthur, who didn't see the gesture. "Well, I guess that makes three of us, since I'm dead, ha ha. In any case, allow me to introduce myself properly," she repeated, gesturing with palms up. "My name is Olivia Hardcastle, and I used to work in this very building. Did you know it used to be a barn?"

"Yes, I heard that," Arthur said. "This bedroom is in the old barn, but my room is in one of the new wings. So is Rose's."

"We used to say, 'You act like you were brought up in a barn,'" Rose said.

"Be nice, Rose," Lois told her. "Go on, Olivia."

"Thank you. My father was the caretaker, and we lived in a cottage on the property. I used to help him care for the farm animals."

"I knew this was once part of an estate," Lois said. "The mansion up the hill is a bed-and-breakfast now."

Olivia frowned. "Bed-and-breakfast?"

"Like an inn," Arthur clarified.

"How interesting," Olivia said. "I have many more questions; for instance, what is this black rectangular object behind me? But first, I want to give you a chance to query me."

Lois and Arthur both started talking. "How did you get here? Where did you come from? Why can we see you? What do you want?"

Olivia gave a high, girlish laugh and tossed her blond curls.

"How old are you?" Arthur asked. "And—I don't mean to pry—but how did you die, and when?"

The three friends leaned forward to listen: Lois in her lounge chair, with her walker nearby; Arthur in a side chair, with his white cane nearby; and Rose in her wheelchair, with her potato chips nearby. I peeked around the corner of the bathroom door.

"I died in 1918 of Spanish flu," Olivia said.

The group gasped in unison. I gasped too, although the humans probably thought I was just throwing up a hairball. A few seconds passed while this revelation from the ghost sank in.

"Oh my God," Lois said, "you poor dear. How old were you when you, uh, passed on?" She looked uncomfortable, no doubt wondering if she was being rude.

"Twenty," Olivia said. "It was sudden. One day I had a cough, the next day I turned blue, and then—I gave up the ghost. Except, not exactly, as you can see." She stifled a giggle with one pale hand.

Rose turned to Lois. "Did she say she turned blue?"

Arthur chimed in. "It was a common sign of Spanish flu, caused by lack of oxygen. I googled it." Arthur was the youngest of the trio at sixty-four, and he had a special computer with a braille reader. He won all the coffee hour trivia contests.

"Googled?" Olivia said.

"It's a long story. Let's just say Arthur is our historian." Lois paused, chewing on a nail. "You know, we're in the middle of a plague of our own right now."

Olivia nodded. "I thought as much. There are several new graves in the cemetery." She pointed out the window, where you could just make out the edge of the memorial park if you craned your neck. But not many residents tried very hard to get a view of it.

"Are you buried there?" Arthur ventured.

"I am, along with a number of other local people who died of the Spanish flu. But not all of them are ghosts."

"How does it work, then, becoming a ghost?" Lois asked. I guessed she was curious about this, now that she was almost ninety.

"It's a long story, like your 'google,'" Olivia said. "No time to explain now."

"Why aren't you still blue?" Rose demanded.

"Rose, be nice," Lois said, giving Olivia an apologetic look. "She has a little trouble keeping up," she whispered.

"On no, that's fine," Olivia reassured them. "One good thing about being a ghost is you don't look like you did when you died. That's an old wives' tale. You actually look like your healthy self." She glanced down at her outfit and shook her head. "Although for some reason, we're all dressed in white. It really washes me out."

Just then, someone shoved on the door. "Uh-oh," Olivia said. "See you tomorrow. We still have so much to accomplish." She swirled to the door, removed the chair, and dematerialized.

Yolanda stumbled into the room. Regaining her balance, she surveyed the three people in front of her. They looked at her blankly, snacks in hand.

"You're still eating?" she said. No one answered. "Okay, I'll be back later." Then she hurried down the hall to deal with her fifteen other residents.

"Phew, that was close," Arthur said.

Lois blew out a puff of air. "Really. What do you think Olivia meant when she said she had more to accomplish?"

Arthur was quiet for a moment. "I don't know. Maybe she has a mission here? I guess we'll find out eventually."

"I was born in 1918," Rose said. Then she sang, "Memories . . ."

* * *

The next day, the three humans were at morning coffee-and-crafts hour. I was lurking under the table, in case someone dropped a cookie. I'm not actually Lois's cat; I just live in the building. So I can go where I please, which is more than some of these poor humans can do.

Anyway, I peeked out and was shocked to see Olivia standing behind

Lois. The ghost tapped Lois on the shoulder. Lois jumped, sloshing coffee on the valentine she was making. Arthur sniffed the air and whispered, "Is Olivia here?"

"Don't worry, friends," Olivia said. "I'm in invisible mode today, so no one can see or hear me but you three."

"What's she doing here?" Rose said in a loud voice, her cookie reduced to crumbs.

"Shhhhhh!" Lois warned. But it was too late. The perky new activity director was on her way over. What was her name again? I couldn't remember. I didn't like her, and I could tell Lois didn't like her either—or her idiotic craft projects. Arthur, being blind, was excused from participating, and so was Rose, because she lacked the manual dexterity to handle scissors. I once heard Lois mutter that they were the lucky ones.

"Is everything all right here?" Miss Perky asked. "Oh dear, Lois, you spilled coffee on your valentine." She dabbed the paper heart with a napkin, but Lois pushed her hand away.

"Okayyy, maybe you'd rather just drink your coffee," Miss Perky said, rolling her eyes and walking to another table where people seemed to be enjoying cutting and pasting paper hearts.

Arthur swiveled his head around, not sure where Olivia was. She placed her hand on his right shoulder. "Here I am, Arthur. I guess showing up now wasn't such a good idea."

Arthur turned toward her voice, shook his head, and whispered, "No, it wasn't. Can you come back this afternoon at the regular time?"

"I think so, but I need to check my schedule," Olivia said. Then she snapped her fingers and—poof—she was gone.

Olivia seemed to be experimenting with different ways to appear and disappear. Well, variety is the spice of life—and death, apparently. No doubt about it: our lives had spiced up in the last few days. The humans had been complaining that they couldn't go out for lunch or have visitors in their rooms because of the pandemic. They especially hated having swabs stuck up their nostrils.

Until this ghost business, my life had been pretty humdrum too.

The high point of my week was Saturday movie night in the recreation room, where they showed movies like *Terminator 2* to keep the residents from dozing off. I'm a fan of old movies too. The other night, Lois and I watched *All About Eve* with Bette Davis.

* * *

That afternoon, Yolanda delivered the snacks—chips, Oreos, and apple juice—and then left in a hurry. I knew Lois had something on her mind, because she was twisting her paper napkin. Then she asked the others, "How do you two feel about Olivia? I mean, I wake up in the morning excited!"

"Me too!" Arthur said without missing a beat. "I can't wait to see her again. Well, you know what I mean."

"How about you, Rose?" Lois asked. "How do you feel?"

We all waited while Rose carefully crunched a potato chip with her front teeth (all the back ones were broken). Just when I thought she hadn't heard the question, Rose spoke up: "Pretty interesting. Life was boring as hell before. Present company excluded."

Sometimes, Rose makes perfect sense.

"I hope she can fit us into her schedule," Arthur said.

"Me too," Lois said, taking a sip of juice with hands that were suddenly unsteady.

I was sitting in the doorway, eavesdropping on the conversation. I'd been telling myself to shape up and not be so skittish when the ghost appeared. So when I felt the vibes in the room change, I stood my ground, even though my instincts were to bolt down the hall. I could tell the humans felt the air stir too, and the two who could see watched the smoky fog seep out from under the window frame until it whirled like a mini tornado and turned into Olivia.

Every hair on my body stood up, but I forced myself to enter and jump onto the desk to get a better view.

"Hello again!" Olivia chirped, drifting in front of the TV. "Sorry about what happened earlier. Very reckless of me."

"No problem," Lois said, although of course it had been. "We're just so glad you could fit us into your schedule."

Arthur rocked in his chair in excitement. "Yeah, we're so glad you came!"

I was glad too, but I like to keep a low profile. I call it going "in-cat-nito." Could other animals see ghosts, or just me?

"I see the cat back there," Olivia said, pointing. "He can see me too; all animals can."

So much for in-cat-nito, I thought, licking my paw in an attempt to act casual.

"So, what's the deal, Olivia?" Arthur said.

"The deal?" I could tell she was puzzled.

"He means, why are you here, and why us?" Lois explained.

"Oh, right," Olivia nodded. "Well, the problem is, I've been neither here nor there for over one hundred years, and I'd like a permanent address. But before I can pass over, my sponsor said my mission was to go back to the place where I died and give someone there a new lease on life. So—here I am."

"Your sponsor? Like in AA?" Arthur asked.

"AA?" Olivia looked puzzled again.

"Never mind," Lois said. "But why us? There are fifty other people living here."

Rose looked up from her empty chip bag and said, "What's going on?"

Lois gave her an annoyed look. "Just listen, OK? This is important."

"Bossy," Rose mumbled.

"So, why haunt us?" Arthur repeated.

Olivia tilted her head and pursed her lips in thought. "I spent some time in invisible mode, hovering near the ceiling, eavesdropping on the other residents and staff. Bunch of bores. You three are the most lively."

Oh yeah? And what am I, chopped liver? I thought, smacking my lips.

"You know, they call us the Fearsome Threesome," Arthur said. "The staff, I mean. At first we were insulted, but now we like it."

"It does have a certain cachet," Olivia remarked. "Oh, I almost forgot—I also chose you to haunt because Rose was born the year I died. The day I died, actually."

"December 13, 1918. Friday the 13th," Rose said. "Bad luck."

"For me, but not for you," Olivia smiled. "I'd say you've had good luck, living to 102."

"I'm not ready to die yet," Rose said, crumpling her empty bag of chips.

"So . . . tell us more about your mission," Lois said, obviously trying to get the conversation back on track. "You're supposed to make someone's life better, is that it?"

"Correct. So, how am I doing so far?" Olivia asked.

No one spoke for a full minute. I stopped licking my fur and pricked up my ears. Finally, Arthur spoke. "You mean the three of us, don't you? You're making our lives better just by showing up here."

"We were just discussing that before you came. How we have something to look forward to now," Lois said, nodding and smiling at everyone. "Wow . . . except . . ." Her smile faded. "Except you'll be going soon, won't you? And you won't be coming back."

"She's dumping us." Rose glared at Olivia.

The ghost bit her lip and avoided their eyes. "I've been waiting one hundred years to get out of that cemetery. Surely you can empathize, with the pandemic lockdowns and all."

The group was quiet again, pondering. "Maybe you could send another ghost?" Arthur suggested. "As long as they're nice like you. Not someone out of a Dickens story with chains and stuff."

"I can check around," Olivia said without much conviction. "But seriously, you three don't need me. Can't you just get on with it? You're friends. You have each other. You're the Fearsome Threesome!" That said, she swirled up to the ceiling and left through the heating vent.

Hasta la vista, baby, I thought. I would've given Olivia the finger if I had one. She had some nerve waltzing in here on her so-called mission and then waltzing off again, leaving my humans sad and depressed when they'd been so happy lately.

"Talk about a grand exit," Rose said. The other two laughed mirthlessly.

Okay, time to break in-cat-nito. I leaped off the desk, trotted across the room, and jumped into Lois's lap. She stroked my fur absently. If my humans needed a new lease on life, I'd give them one. Clearing my throat, I said in my best Bette Davis imitation, "Fasten your seatbelts, it's going to be a bumpy night."

And that's when the Fearsome Threesome became the Fearsome Foursome.

Mike Vreeland
Late to the Party

I'M A PRIVATE PERSON. I DON'T DO *ME* VERY WELL. I don't enjoy small talk or mingling. (I just realized I started the last three sentences with "I"—four including this one. So much for not doing me.) I didn't use to be this way, but life throws curves. Hairpin turns, actually.

On Saturday, my friend Rick called to invite me to a Labor Day bash at his family's lake house. His parents retired a few years ago and planned to spend summers there, but they rarely go. Rick has the place to himself, and he's converted it from a summers-only cottage to his insulated year-round home.

"Who's going to be there?" I asked. Not that it mattered who. It was the number of people that worried me. Big gatherings I can handle. I can blend in for a while and slip out without a fuss. Intimate gatherings cause anxiety. The lack of escape, short of feigning illness, is unbearable.

"A bunch of people," Rick replied. "Some people from where I work, friends of mine you'd get along with great. We're having steaks and burgers, clams and wings. People are bringing salads and junk food. It's a party. I'm providing a few cases of artisan beer, but we'll have wine and whatever else people bring."

"Anyone I know?" I looked at myself in the bathroom mirror as I spoke, wishing I hadn't canceled my last couple of haircuts. My buzz cut was looking shaggy.

"You know me," Rick replied. "Besides, Alan, these are great people. You'll love 'em." Rick was always Mr. Ray of Sunshine. I've known him for a couple of years, since we met at a grief support group. His sister died unexpectedly of a brain tumor. My fiancée died in a car accident. A driver fell asleep at the wheel and crossed the line into her lane. Rick and I were both in a bad state when we met, but somehow, he came to terms with his sister's death and moved on. Now, he says he wants to live each day to the fullest. I haven't been that fortunate. There are days when I barely want to live.

"You still there?" Rick asked.

"Yeah, sorry."

"You don't need to let me know this second. By tomorrow, though. OK?"

"Sure, thanks."

"Cool." Rick hung up.

I lay back on my sofa and pulled a blanket over me. I needed the world to go away so I could think. I recalled the layout of Rick's lake house. I'd been there several times helping Rick fix things up, but it had only been the two of us. The house was small, but it had a large patio, a modest but tidy lawn beyond that, and a wooden L-shaped dock that extended several feet out onto the lake. When I was there, Rick had a rowboat tied up to the dock. I could take the boat out and be both at the party and alone. A Schrödinger party.

Rick was right. I should have kept up with the grief support group, but I wasn't feeling any better after three months, and Rick was. At the time, I took it as a sign I should do something different if I was to move on, as they say. But move on to what? Nobody ever explains that part. My fiancée and I had plans. I can't move on with those plans.

Maybe Rick had an easier time because it was just his sister, while I lost the love of my life. That sounds cruel. Of course, he loved his sister. Now I feel bad for even attempting to compare our grief. I recall the grief counselor drilling into our heads at the start of every meeting that everyone's journey through grief is unique. There are days when mine feels like an endless trip through a deep, narrow canyon.

Maybe Rick had an easier time because he is older. He's about thirty-five, a whole ten years older. Maybe in those ten years, people gain wisdom that helps them deal with loss. If only I could sleep for ten years and wake up with that wisdom. Then maybe I could move on. After two years of living with this weight, I've barely budged.

Except for interacting with the cashier at Winthrop Food Mart and the neighbor's beagle, I haven't had much in-person contact with the world all summer. All spring and summer, to be honest. Programming is not a job that requires much face time. Clients converse through email and pay online. An introvert's dream.

I guess that's what I am now. An introvert. There are millions of introverts in the world. There is nothing wrong with them. It's a personality type. Now that I'm an introvert, I'm just one of them. There's nothing wrong with me.

Except there is.

Rick knows it. I know it. I'm just not sure what to do about it.

For a moment I want to be the old me. I decide to go to the party.

I leave Rick a message. He texts back: *Bring your swimsuit.*

A fresh round of panic hits me in the gut. I've made a commitment. Hard to back out now.

I take a deep breath, get up off the sofa, and dig through my dresser for my suit. I own two: a blue Speedo from my college swim team days and red board shorts from my summers as a lifeguard at the town pool.

I opt for the board shorts. I don't plan on racing anyone across the lake. I wonder if I could even make it across the lake. I've kept up a workout routine at home, so I still look and feel fit, but I haven't been in the water in over two years. Maybe it's time.

* * *

I glance at the clock on the dashboard. I pull into the Food Mart parking lot, walk into the store, pick up a small cheese platter and a six-pack of hard lemonade, and pay. The six-pack was planned. The cheese platter looked good as I passed the deli.

I return to the car and look at the clock again. The party started an hour ago. It should be safe to arrive and slip in without much notice.

When I pull onto Rick's street, a winding lane through a vacation community, cars are parked along the sides, making the driving lane barely a car's width.

I find a spot to park without too much trouble, pick up the platter and six-pack, and close the car door with my hip.

I walk through the open front door and across the crowded living room to the sliding doors onto the patio. I make room for the platter on the food table and put the six-pack in one of the coolers of iced beverages.

"Alan," calls Rick. I turn to see his head peering over the raised lid of a massive grill on the side of the patio. Wisps of smoke rise around his head. If he wasn't wearing such a huge grin and a brightly colored Hawaiian shirt, he might look demonic. Instead, he looks cherubic.

"Sorry I'm late," I respond.

"Better late than never," he says waving for me to come over. "I want you to meet some of my friends."

I nod, and Rick proceeds to name those around him. I shake a lot of hands as he takes me around to pretty much everyone on the patio. At this point, I don't think I'll remember a single name.

Then he takes me into the living room. He must be tired of introductions by now. He calls out, "Hey everybody. This is my friend, Alan. Everybody introduce themselves."

They do, but in such rapid succession, their names and faces are a blur. It's likely I'll not see them again, so I tell myself that remembering their names doesn't matter.

People return to their conversations. No one makes a move to include me, so I head back to the food table and help myself to some vegetables and dip, and some cheese from my platter. I guess it was a good choice. About a third of it has been eaten already.

I sit with my small plate in a lawn chair next to two women chatting like they are alone. One is thinking of leaving her husband, but only if she gets to keep the Ferrari; otherwise she'll stay and make his life hell until he agrees.

In my mind I'm thinking, Give her the Ferrari! I wonder if he even knows.

The shade has crept away from my chair and the sun is blazing. The lake looks so inviting. I decide to walk back to my car and grab my swim trunks and towel.

On my way, I notice a young woman heading toward the party. An expensive-looking camera hangs from her neck, and she is carrying a small bakery box. She looks down as we get near, her face hidden behind shoulder-length dark hair. No eye contact. I say hello anyway. She doesn't respond. She's late to the party. My kind of person.

The bathroom is empty, so I change into my trunks and then make my way to the dock with my towel in hand. A couple of guys have the boat out a few yards beyond the dock and are swimming near it, but otherwise the water is mine.

I remove my shirt, dive in, and relish the cool sensation on my skin. I do a quick crawl down the lake, turning before the next owner's dock. All that muscle memory has returned, and I realize how much I enjoy the water.

A slow backstroke brings me back to Rick's dock. From my vantage point in the lake, the party seems lively. Sounds like everyone is having a good time. I can hear Rick's laugh among the many voices.

I realize I'm the exception. Not that I'm not having a good time, but I'm not doing much mingling out here in the lake. I promised Rick I would try.

As I climb onto the dock, one of the guys at the boat calls to me, so I walk to the outer end.

"Are you a lifeguard?" he asks.

Sees my red shorts, I guess. "Not on duty," I reply. They laugh.

I turn and walk back to the lawn to retrieve my towel and shirt, but as I do, I look up to see a woman with her camera aimed toward me.

Without thinking, I smile and wave.

As I'm drying off, she approaches. I recognize her. The dark-haired woman I passed on the way to my car.

"I hope you don't mind," she says, her words sounding like an apology. "Your silhouette against the light on the water caught my eye."

"As long as it was just my silhouette and not my haven't-been-to-the-gym-in-a-while body," I say, half joking. I realize I still have my shirt in my hand, so I slip it on.

"Mostly," she replies, a little blush coloring her cheeks. "I can delete them."

"No worries." I'm not sure where to take the conversation after that, so I opt for action. "Care to get a burger?"

"Sure," she says. The awkward moment has passed.

I squeeze through the group at the grill, and Rick sets me up with two fresh burgers on sturdy paper plates. We meet at the condiment table, which is loaded with every possible burger add-on. Lettuce, tomatoes, mushrooms, ketchup, mustard, mayo, and some things I can't identify. I spy the sliced onions but decide to pass on them for now. Onions and conversation don't mix.

We find a shady spot with two empty lawn chairs and sit with our plates on our laps. We chat between bites.

"You're a good swimmer," she says.

"Thanks. I swam in college." I realize she must have been watching me before my silhouette on the dock, but I keep that knowledge to myself. "Do you swim?"

"Not today. But sometimes. I've mastered the doggie paddle and do an adequate American crawl. I do enjoy myself, though."

I think I should offer her lessons, but I stop myself. I'm so out of the swing of socializing. She seems nice. I don't want to screw this up. I reply, "Enjoyment is the key. Why do it otherwise?"

She laughs. "I like that philosophy—"

Our conversation is interrupted by a scream. "Help! He's choking!"

We look up toward the patio. Through the assortment of legs, I see someone on his knees, holding his throat.

"He's turning blue!" a woman's voice cries. "Call 911."

I run up to the patio and push my way through. I recognize Rick's Hawaiian shirt on the crouching figure.

"Rick," I shout. "I'm gonna do the Heimlich on you."

Rick looks up and nods, his red eyes pleading.

I stand him back up with the help of another guy, wrap my arms around him, and do several abdominal thrusts. Finally, the offending morsel flies out of his mouth. He takes several deep breaths, coughs, and clears his throat.

"Thanks," he whispers. I sit him in a chair.

A big cheer goes up. It takes me a minute to realize it's for me. I assumed they were cheering because Rick was okay and the party could continue.

I stay with Rick until the EMTs arrive and check him out, but by that time, he's his old cheerful self. If he is hurting, he's not showing it.

"Now I'm really glad you came to the party," Rick says, patting me on the shoulder.

"Me, too," I reply. *For this and another reason*, I say to myself.

I start back to my lawn chair, but the young woman I was chatting with is gone. I look around. I realize I never found out her name. With my luck, I'll bet it's *Cinderella*. It's midnight somewhere.

I walk around the lawn, down by the dock, and through the house. While I'm inside, I might as well get out of my wet suit.

I grab my clothes out of the hallway closet where I stashed them. The bathroom door opens and out steps Cinderella, or whatever her name is.

"There you are," I say. I immediately regret sounding like I was looking for her. "I was just about to change." I hold up my clothes.

"It's all yours."

"I'll only be a minute." I close the door, change, and wrap my damp suit in my towel to ditch in the closet. I check my hair in the mirror and step into the hallway.

I guess I shouldn't have expected her to be standing there waiting. Now I'll have to look for her again.

She wasn't far. Standing in the patio doorway.

"Want to continue our conversation?" I ask.

"Sure."

"Our chairs are still available."

"Great."

"We were never properly introduced," I say. "I'm Alan."

"I knew that from all the people talking after you saved Rick. But nice to meet you," she says, holding out her hand in mock formality. "I'm Cindy."

My brain does a double-take. Cinderella? "That's not short for something, is it?"

"Nope. Plain Cindy."

"Plain isn't a word I'd use," I respond. Self-doubt rushes in. Am I being too obvious? My brain kicks itself.

Cindy blushes and places a hand on my arm. "Thanks. And that was awesome, by the way, how you saved Rick."

"Part of my lifeguard training. I learned that people are more likely to choke at the beach than they are to drown."

Rick is making his way toward us. "Say, you two. I see you've already met. That's great."

I'm thinking, *Was Rick trying to set me up*? I should be annoyed, but I'm not.

Cindy looks puzzled. "But this is Alan. You wanted me to meet Wyatt somebody."

Rick grins. "Cindy Newman, meet Alan Wyatt."

Cindy and I just look at each other and start laughing.

Now it's Rick's turn to look puzzled. "I guess I'm the one that's late to the party."

"Better late than never," I tease.

"Enjoy," Rick says as he walks off, shaking his head.

I turn back to Cindy. "Rick never mentioned meeting someone."

"He told me you probably wouldn't even show."

"He knows me too well," I laugh.

"Why wouldn't you? Show, I mean."

"Long story."

"I've got time." She smiles and settles into her chair.

By Dax Shadowalker, as presented by Susan Martha Thompson

Life Without Time

I CONSIDER MYSELF FORTUNATE to have lived on the Southern Ute Reservation in southwestern Colorado among my people, who are made of earth, wind, water, and fire. Each morning, as they met the day, Mother and Father stood before the rising sun and thanked the Great Spirit for the goodness in their lives. This goodness included the love they held for each other; their two strong sons—myself, Dax Bearcat, and my younger brother, Dominic Grayowl; Grandmother and Grandfather, who taught them the ways of our people; and the abundance which greeted them as they walked the earth.

I learned to do the same. Less fortunate souls might not know if morning would bring a full or empty bowl. Not all rest their heads at night on soft pillows. Too many sit in the ashes of what could be. Our parents taught us what blessing meant. We were fortunate, they said, to live in the land of flowered meadows and snow-covered peaks among family, friends, home, cattle who grazed, and hawks who watched.

I, too, watched. I considered in a serious manner each small chance to learn about my world and that of others. I noted the newborn butterfly, the early song of spring on feathered wings, the crispness of the air when sleep beckoned and when nomads began their journey toward promised warmth. I gave each moment its worth so that I might be worthy. It was with this mind that I began to understand the things that keep us whole.

* * *

I think back to when I was still a child, having walked the earth under eleven harvest moons. I looked forward to the twelfth year of my life with many expectations and also some fear. I would be sent to live alone for twelve days in the desert so that I might leave behind that childhood. This is a custom still practiced by our people in a world that often ignores tradition. I heard stories of boys wandering for many days with little sense in their heads and not enough water or food. When my time came, I lived with the coyotes and lizards I learned to call brothers. I ate and drank what the land offered. I breathed and slept like the crow that sits on a branch and the jackrabbit finding warmth in its burrow. My parents and grandparents had taught me about the ways of the desert and how to live within its clutches. After completing my journey of aloneness and visions, I returned home and was looked upon as a man by my people.

Until that time, however, I was an observer left to my wishes and suspicions. Duties done, I could play. Or sit at the fire and hear again the stories of the Great Ones who fought for us to remain who we are as a nation. I liked to create my own stories with little hope of a listener except for my dog, Ahawi, with his ever attentive ears. In my tales, I wove not only legends, but often what I believed to be subtle truths.

One such story concerned my father, who was an artist. He often drove far from home into the desert to spend a day, sometimes a week, recreating what he saw using oil paints on canvas. He offered for my brother or me to accompany him. Dominic had no interest. I had my backpack full and ready. With little else to do apart from roaming among the cactuses and buttes, I spent hours watching my father. I noticed that, after he found the right spot and had his tools at hand, this man, whom I thought I knew so well, seemed to leave who he was behind and become a creator entwined in the magic and magnificence of his vision. The questions I longed to ask him remained unspoken. He took no notice of me or the world, or anything beyond his brush and the beauty he was imitating. Later, as we sat in darkness warming ourselves at the fire, he smiled and called it a good day. I wondered about what I had witnessed when he seemed to be distant and unreachable. I asked myself: "What was that?"

Another story of mine was about one spring when our parents took

Dominic and me to Taos, New Mexico, to visit Father's brother and his family. We planned to celebrate the vernal equinox at the ancient houses of the people who lived there many years ago. While at our family's home, my aunt took us into a back room that held a great wooden structure I knew to be a loom. We had learned about them in school. On the loom was the beginning of what looked like a large rug with a many-colored design on it. Aunt Beta said it was fashioned with the colors of the Navajo Nation, where she lived as a girl. My family left to go into town, but I stayed as she sat and began to do things with the fibers in different directions. As she directed what she called the warp and the woof, I watched her have an experience similar to the one I observed of my father in the desert. She began to hum a tune I had never heard. It sounded like the wind of the mountains whispering through the pines. Her face looked serene and her lips were set in a small smile. In silence I sat and closed my eyes, thinking, and hoping, she might somehow take me with her.

My last tale was about the time Father took me to the home of the Paiutes. As we traveled west across southern Utah, we drove through the Ute Mountain Ute lands. These were our people who decided not to cooperate with the government. They refused to divide their land for private ownership or believe in promised money. Their customs and culture remained traditional in most ways.

After driving for several hours, we stopped at a harvest celebration. When asked why we traveled so far toward the setting sun, Father answered: "To see a friend." He said nothing more.

"Sharing too much is often regretted," Father told me later. "Daniel was my roommate at Fort Lewis College in Durango," he added. "Native people who are at least one-quarter Indian and are enrolled in a recognized tribe can attend tuition-free. Students come from throughout the southwestern United States for their education. Daniel studied the fine arts and now sells his creations with much success."

This was the most Father had ever talked with me that I could remember. I smiled, thinking this trip was a very good idea.

As we neared Daniel's home, I saw smoke rising behind a small building. Father assured me his friend would explain. After refreshments, we were guided to the small building. In the corner, among several heavy wooden tables, were two pottery wheels. One had a pedal; the other had an electric cord plugged into a nearby outlet.

"The smoke you see is from this kiln." He pointed to a large structure made of bricks that looked like an oven. "I dig the clay from the river bank and, after forming it, fire it in here," Daniel continued. "It's fueled with wood that has to be added over several hours until the temperature is right. Then, after a while, it slowly cools down." He took a large clump of red clay from a table and showed it to me. "This is what I use for the wood kiln. You never know how pots will come out, but they're usually unique and interesting. I also have this electric kiln. Here's the gray clay that I buy for firing in it. Most of the ceramics I sell come out of this one. It's much easier to control and the results are more predictable. I didn't tell you about the underglazing or glazing of the pots, but that's for another time. Would you like to watch me throw a pot on a wheel, Dax?"

I nodded, and Father excused himself to drive into town and buy some groceries for a special dish he wanted to make for supper. Daniel sat at his electric wheel and began his work. Once again I watched. And, again, the artist seemed to travel somewhere. But this time, I felt like I was floating along with him.

Four hours later, Father joined us. "Dinner's ready," he announced.

Daniel and I stared at each other. I could tell by his knowing look he was aware of what I was thinking: How? Where was the time? And where did you go, Daniel? Did I go with you?

* * *

Today, many years later, I sit at my own pottery wheel. I check to be sure I have all the tools I will need for the first step: my bucket of water, sponges, ribs, wire. As I lay my hands on my wedged clay, I begin my work. The things that come of it will say much about who I am. I have that to give to my world.

I learned that a precious part of living a life built on time is spending some of it without that distraction. Still, the question of my youth persists. Is this elusive part of life, when time escapes us, no more than focusing on what we're doing? Or is it something else? The brush, the loom, the wheel—I suspect they know.

Though I continue to be left wondering about the truth of all this, what I do know is : each time I allow myself to go there, I, too, become a creator who leaves his body to transform into that person who understands himself.

Story Note:

As the first Native American officer in the Park City, Utah, Police Department, Dax Shadowalker reminisced about the days before he settled into the responsibilities of adulthood. In this story, he introduced himself as a young man living on the Southern Ute Reservation, busied with the work of discovering his world. Leaving home for college and eventual employment leads him into a life of unexpected adventure, tragedy, and love. You can join him on that journey as the main character in the soon-to-be-published novel Big Red Sun, authored by Susan Martha Thompson.

Laurie A. Guzda

Name Your Days

NORA CLIMBED INTO HER BIG COMFY BED and nestled under the well-worn flannel sheets and overstuffed down comforter. She propped her pillow so she could sit comfortably as she grabbed the diary and pen sitting on the nightstand. Adjusting her glasses, she slid her hand along the bottom to find the piece of ribbon used to bookmark today's date. It was a five-year diary, but Nora only used one line to name her day. She could use this book for twenty years. She re-read the titles from the previous three years on this day: *Why Not Me? A Cardinal at My Window. Drop of Reflection.*

It was hard to believe that she was starting her fourth year of naming her days. It began after Ben Burdick's memorial service.

The rabbi spoke about Ben with such fondness. Ben was a beautiful man who died too young. He was a dentist, husband, and father who was involved in community theater. At first Ben only did box office props, and sometimes helped with costumes. His wife and daughter were the actors in the family. But, like most community theaters, it was hard to find men to perform. So Ben was recruited.

His wife and daughter laughed at the rabbi's last comment. It seemed they, and those in attendance, remembered Ben's resistance to the spotlight. There had to be close to four hundred people in that room. The large geometric design of the stained glass reflected hues of red, yellow, and blue that danced over the faces of the laughing crowd.

Nora knew that if his wife and daughter could laugh at a time like this, then they would be okay. Of course, she knew, they were very sad at the moment, but that little light of laughter was a strong indicator that their relationship was healthy and they would heal over time. These two women had each other to help them through.

Nora's attention was drawn back to the rabbi after another burst of laughter. He was talking about Ben's first few productions, which were not very good. He was not very good. But he wanted to be. He worked hard to be a better actor. His last role was Murray Burns in A Thousand Clowns. And in that role, he was good. Very good.

As the rabbi spoke so eloquently about Ben and his passion for family, work, and the theater, he got choked up at the mention of Ben's role as Murray Burns.

The rabbi took a deep breath before he continued: "During the production, Ben learned of the diagnosis that would shorten his life." You could hear sniffles and then the sound of someone trying to politely blow their nose.

The rabbi went on, "There's a beautiful monologue in the play where Murray says, 'I gotta know what day it is. I gotta know what's the name of the game and what the rules are without anyone else telling me. Ya gotta own your own days and name 'em, each one of 'em, every one of 'em, or else the years go right by and none of them belong to you.'"

Nora sat silently in the synagogue pew listening to those words. They landed hard. On her way home she stopped to purchase a diary so she could begin to name her days.

* * *

It was a wet Wednesday in November. Thankfully, it was mild, almost balmy. Nora wore a plain white dress that hung loosely on her thin frame. The beige and white shawl would keep her warm enough. She grabbed an umbrella, just to be safe. She drove the eighty-five miles to Saugerties, New York.

She got out of the car and decided that she didn't need the umbrella. The rain slowed, then stopped. As the clouds cleared, a rainbow appeared. Nora took a moment to appreciate the beauty of the colors, then smiled as she followed the path to the building ahead.

Everyone was dressed in white. Nora held her lavender-scented white lace handkerchief to her nose as she approached the casket and laid a bouquet of flowers from Trader Joe's on top of the many other floral offerings. She had read that Buddhist ceremonies often cremate the body days after death, so no embalming is necessary. Today was the day for Achara Ram, and not a day too soon as far as Nora was concerned.

The service began with music, chanting, and dance. It was somber but pleasing at the same time. Several people then got up to speak. Most were Achara's coworkers from Phoenix Labs. It seemed more than a little ironic that Achara was the supervisor for the company's car safety testing program. After all, nothing is going to protect you when you get hit by an eighteen-wheeler head-on. The truck driver suffered a mild concussion and walked away from the accident.

Achara's body was carried into the crematorium. Women were not allowed inside. Instead, the remaining crowd moved outside and down the hill. They headed toward the river. Sweet cakes and tea were served. The music and chanting began again. A priest, or a monk—Nora wasn't quite sure which—with a brass incense burner moved from person to person whispering a prayer while fanning the sweet-smelling smoke to cleanse each one. It was an earthy scent not unlike burning leaves, but sweeter.

More than two hours had passed when the chanting and conversation was interrupted by the soft sound of a drum slowly beating in the distance. A procession of men, each carrying bundles, walked solemnly from the top of the hill to join the others. They lined up along the river near the beach where access was easiest. Each guest stepped up to receive a small leaf bowl that held a scoop of Achara's ashes, still warm, covered with flowers and topped with a tea light. Each was then lit by a man holding an ornate, long-tipped lighter. A small polished stone was placed in the wax of the candle.

Each guest carefully walked to the beach, cupping their precious gift, kneeled at the water as they offered a prayer, and sent the little flower boat floating down the river.

Nora watched as they made their offerings. She wondered what kind of prayers they had said. It was hard to tell what they were feeling. Everyone seemed so stoic. Nora didn't cry. She had never met Achara. She hadn't known of her existence until she read about the accident. When it was her turn, Nora whispered, "Hi, my name is Nora. You don't know me. I just came to wish you safe travels to the other side. Oh, and say hello to Sam. Thanks."

By the time Nora arrived home, she was exhausted. With barely enough energy, she lifted the heavy diary. She named the day White Lace Lavender and Death. She erased that and wrote Achara's River Styx & Stone. It sounded happier to Nora.

* * *

Nora enjoyed attending funerals and memorials. It was easy to blend in and observe how many ways there are to celebrate. She could tell a lot about a person by their service and those they left behind. No two services were the same. Even in the same religion, each was unique, though she did find similarities. And there was usually a good meal to be had. At least something sweet and delicious. She could sometimes fit a week's worth of treats in her bag.

Nora scanned her usual resources looking for her next event. She knew she had found it when she read about Norman Spivek.

Unsure of what to wear for Norman's Celebration of Life ceremony, Nora was glad she decided to don the blue wig. Normally a blue wig would cause one to stand out in a crowd, but not this crowd. In this circle, Norman was known as Puff - Puff the Magic Drag Queen.

Nora sat on a barstool next to the railing in the rear of the dimly lit cabaret theater. As she adjusted herself on the stool a voice announced, "Everyone please find a seat. The show will be starting in ten minutes."

A huge man sat on the stool next to Nora. He was well over six feet tall and looked to weigh in close to four hundred pounds with biceps the size of Nora's head. He turned to her and smiled, showing the absence of several teeth as he said with a lisp, "Are you thaving thith thool for thumone?"

"No, it was waiting for you."

He stuck out his meaty mitt of a hand. "I'm Mista Fista the Oga Eata."

"Wow. That's a mouthful! Mister Fister the Ogre Eater—what kind of name is that?"

"Ith my westhling name. Mosth people jus call me Oga."

Nora shook his hand. "I'm Nora. Nice to meet you."

Just then, a beautiful woman smartly dressed came up to Ogre. "They need you to help carry Puff. Zouzou is waiting by the back door."

Ogre got up, nodded at the woman, and smiled at Nora. "Enthoy the thow."

Nora was a little surprised by the deep-throated voice of the woman. Is she a woman? Does it matter? Nora didn't care; it's all just costume. What's the difference really if you want to wear a suit or a dress? We all end up as dust in the end.

The woman took the stool vacated by Ogre. "Ogre's a sweet guy, just one too many jolts to the head, if you know what I mean. The first time I met him was when Puff body-slammed him so hard he crawled around the ring looking for Nancy Reagan." She laughed.

"Puff was a wrestler?"

"Oh my, yes. Part-time drag queen, part-time wrestler. He was known as the Death Doula because he wanted to help his victims to cross over comfortably." She laughed louder. "I don't think he was ever comfortable in his skin as a woman or a man. Some people are like that, you know? Did he accidentally overdose or was it intentional? We'll never know, will we?"

Nora was about to respond when the house lights dimmed. The stage lights cast a glow as a disco diva drag queen appeared in a spotlight, center stage. She wore a mirrored dress, and her pink beehive was at least two feet high. She began singing "I Will (Not) Survive."

The show lasted about an hour. All the numbers were vibrant and full of life. They were bawdy and completely inappropriate. It was deliciously perfect. The house lights came up as several large individuals, including Ogre, carried an enormous pine box onto the stage. It was placed standing, like a wooden phone booth. The crowd looked on nervously as a Cher look-alike opened the box, Vanna White style, to reveal a life-size wax figure of Puff. The audience erupted into applause as she announced that Puff would forever greet all who enter.

Nora walked home still singing disco songs. It was fun. She wished she had known Norman while he was alive. He was loved very much. Nora was comfortable among these open-minded and open-hearted people who liked to dress up, sing, and dance. She wondered why that wasn't enough for Puff. Was his overdose accidental or intentional? Why be an addict when you had so much love?

Once home, Nora pulled out her book and named the day Death Doula. She erased it and wrote Last Dance. She erased that and wrote Die Like a Drag Queen.

Nora flipped through the pages, reading her titles, remembering each and every day. She had attended so many services and memorials. There was Catch and Release of Fisherman Fred, Too Young to Be Taken, Darkness and Despair of the Mother Left Behind.

She had never met any of them, yet she felt like they were all part of her family now. There are so many ways to celebrate death. There are ceremonies to help the spirit on its journey. There are traditions to comfort those mourning. There are even companies that help you plan a unique event, and other companies that provide alternate burial choices. You can have your loved one turned into a stone set in jewelry. Fred the Fisherman's ashes were mixed into concrete along with a few personal items and shaped into a habitat for underwater creatures. His loved ones were given his coordinates in Long Island Sound so they could send offerings his way while passing by on occasion.

As Nora considered all the things that are available when someone dies, there are so many more that are not.

What there is not? Answers. No answers as to why people are taken away when they are. No answers on how to lessen the pain. No answers about where they go. Are they safe? Are they happy? Are they hungry? Are they warm enough?

We are all born and we will all die. We don't remember our birth and we don't know when death will come. Still, it's not a subject often discussed at the dinner table. For some cultures it's even taboo to speak of the dead, while others embrace death as a natural rite of passage. A passage to where? Nora felt that nothing we are told truly makes sense. How can anything in life really make sense unless we have a deeper respect and understanding of death?

* * *

Dressed all in black and sporting a substantial wide-brimmed hat dotted with silk flowers that might be zinnias, Nora took a seat just about in the center of the small Baptist church, in a pew under a stained glass window of the baby Jesus hugging a lamb.

The choir entered and took their places on the risers. The musical director was a slight wisp of a woman. She looked to be in her eighties, maybe nineties. She slowly tucked a loose strand of her gray, wiry hair behind her ear. She looked so fragile. She nodded to the choir and placed her hands gently upon the keys. She took a moment to close her eyes and steady her hands. Suddenly, on the first bang of the keys, the choir erupted into "Down By the Riverside." She didn't look fragile anymore. She was a force of nature.

People were standing in the seats, arms raised high, praising the lord. They danced in the aisle. The Reverend Malcom Jeter greeted people as he danced his way to the altar. After many Alleluias and Amens, people took their seats.

Reverend Jeter spoke about death in a warm, loving way. It was home. It was being with Jesus. The choir sang "The Sweet By and By," "How Great Thou Art," and a rendition of "Amazing Grace" that had everyone sobbing and pounding their chests. It was extraordinary. The energy in that small church could fill an ocean.

The reverend spoke about Madeline Jefferson. "She was a wife, a mother, and a grandmother. She loved to sing, and she was known throughout the county for her pecan pie. For over forty years she was an active community leader with our neighbor, the Prosperity Baptist Church.

"Madeline, along with five fellow church members, was singing and praying, much like us here today. How could she, or any of them, have known that day would be the day that they would meet the good Lord? That's why we live each day ready to meet our maker. That's why Madeline and the others were ready when that young, deeply disturbed boy, haunted by demons within, decided to enter our sister church and spray those blessed souls with bullets of ignorance and hate."

Nora shivered at those last words spoken. The randomness and unfairness of it all.

The reverend spoke more about the fragility of life. "It is so important to live each day the best that you can. Say I love you more. Dance more. Let your heart sing loud. Because when it's your turn to go, that's what people will remember about you. That's what will inspire them to more greatly laugh, sing, and dance. To love."

The reverend ended with an invitation to gather in the church hall for a meal and to celebrate Madeline and the others who died together on that fateful day. The choir sang "When the Saints Go Marching In," and everyone danced their way over to the hall.

Nora was exiting the bathroom when a man in a wheelchair parked himself in front of her.

"Excuse me," Nora said as she tried to move around him. But he moved to block her way.

"I know who you are," he said.

Nora tried to move around him.

"Please." he said. "I know it's hard, but we only have each other. Who else is there?"

"I can't." As she tried to push past him, Nora's dress caught on the edge of the wheelchair. She tried to rip it free. He grabbed her hand and held it tight.

"I'm like you. I'm a funeral tourist too," said the man in the wheelchair with a snide laugh.

"You are nothing like me," Nora offered back softly, unable to meet his eyes as she pulled her hand from his and tried to release her dress.

"I know that your son died in your arms. I know that your husband died trying to protect both of you."

Shaking her head, she repeated, "No. No. No."

The man continued. "Why would anyone think that taking your child to a matinee of Coco two days before Christmas would end in a such a tragic way? That boy had no right to be anywhere near an AK-47. He was more than, what did they say . . . mentally unbalanced?"

"I can't," Nora whispered again.

"Mine wasn't a matinee. Mine was a parade. We—my wife and I—were sitting at a café. I wanted a coffee. She wanted to get off her feet. She was eight months pregnant with our first child. It all happened so fast. The car careened down the parade route while that sonuvabitch in the passenger seat fired wildly at the crowd." His eyes watered at the memory.

He looked up into Nora's eyes. "He was laughing. I could see his face and he was laughing. I see that face over and over again. Laughing." He fell silent.

Nora ripped her dress free from the wheelchair. But she didn't move past the man. They looked at each other with great sadness in their eyes.

"Please, can you help me outside? I need some air."

Nora pushed his chair down the side ramp to a bench by the cemetery. She engaged the brake on his chair. She sat next to him on the bench. They sat in silence for some time before Nora spoke. "I like going to services. I find comfort in the sadness. I'm fascinated by people, however they choose to celebrate. Celebrate. That's such a funny word for death."

"Funny, isn't it? I remember when I heard about another shooting. I felt like I had to go and pay my respects, like I was part of this thing now." Thinking about his words, the man in the wheelchair nervously picked at his cuticles. "While I was sitting there, I realized that I needed to be there. For me. I needed to be there just for me. It felt like the only place I could breathe. I also thought that I might be losing my mind." He continued to pick at his cuticles until he drew blood. He quickly put his finger in his mouth to stanch the bleeding.

"I get it," said Nora. "It's a weight that never leaves. I carry it everywhere I go, every day, every minute, except when it's someone else's turn. I'm sad for them. I truly am. But through their sadness, mine is temporarily put on hold, you know?" Nora stared into the distance.

"I tried a couple of support groups but couldn't be part of any more 'whose shooting was worse' conversations. As if it was a competition? I didn't mean to startle you or just appear like that. I just needed, well, I just needed to sit with someone who understands. Don't need to talk about it. Don't need any help to remember. Just needed to know that I'm not alone. Just need to know that I'm still alive, that something matters. Something like . . . hope?"

They sat together in silence for a long time. It was getting dark. An older woman approached them. "Rodrigo, there you are. I've been looking for you. It's time for us to go home."

"I'll be right there, mama."

Nora and Rodrigo held each other's hands tightly in a ball between them. They looked at each other and spoke volumes without uttering a word. A tear ran down Rodrigo's cheek as he pulled their hands to his forehead before releasing to wipe the tear away. After one last all-knowing look at Nora, he turned his chair to go and join his mother.

Soon after, Nora went back inside. She stood at the door watching all the people. They were singing, dancing, laughing. They were sharing love. She envied them. Nora turned and left.

Nora thought about the day as she washed her face, brushed her teeth, and threw on her favorite nightgown. She thought about the service and the vibrant music. She thought about the reverend. How hard it must be to constantly comfort other people in their pain. Who comforts him? She thought about Puff and Achara and Ben. She thought about her husband, Charlie, and their beautiful boy, Sam. Oh, how she missed her boy. She missed Charlie. Is there a way through the pain?

She climbed into her big comfy bed and nestled under the well-worn flannel sheets and overstuffed down comforter. She propped her pillow so she could sit comfortably as she grabbed the diary and pen sitting on the nightstand. Picking up her book, turning to today's date, she thought about what to name today. Something was different. Rodrigo had opened something in her. She felt outed as some kind of pathetic pervert playing with people's pain. But it was her pain that exists in every moment. The truth of it all so easily accessible yet living constantly just on the edge of everything. It's life in no man's land.

Wiping away a tear, Nora picked up her pencil and wrote her name for today.

Hope.

Elaine Leet
Ready or Not

Nu-A-P-P's Story

WE MOVED IN SILENCE, IN SECRET, lest the natives discover us and attack. Indigenous people were few here, but the odds of discovery were still greater than we liked. The night was dark, the moon hidden in the planet's shadow. Wisps of vapor dulled the starlight. My child moaned in my arms.

We had been traveling for months in a vain attempt to escape a mutated virus that killed most of our people. My oldest daughter had died. My son, though still walking on his own, struggled to breathe as the virus assaulted his system. Now, even as I cradled my baby girl in my arms, Death sapped the life from her.

In a desperate attempt to save them, we had journeyed to a desolate piece of land on an alien world where ancient ruins of once-powerful volcanoes surrounded us. Our scientists told us specific flora rooted in the shallow soil might hold the cure for our disease. These native shrubs, growing over molten rock enriched in iron and magnesium and depleted in silica, were thought to support the fungi that could restore my children's health—and hope for our people.

My husband dug the dry ground, exposing a network of roots below the sparse plant life. Lowering his face to the soil, my son inhaled deeply and then looked up in relief as his breathing improved. He filled his pockets with the soil.

We removed my frail daughter's cloaking and placed it on the ground nearby. Too weak to even open her eyes, my child's breaths came in small gasps. Her father placed her among the roots.

Then came the red light flickering. It wandered among the rocks and sparse plant life. Footfalls crunched on the cinder ground, followed by a muffled metallic sound. Silence returned and the light went dark. Hidden by our cloaks, we joined hands around the shallow hollow where my daughter lay. I whispered the ancient rite of my people, begging the universe to spare my child. Later, a sound rose from the opening of a cave, a melody strange—at times raw and at times aching—matching my grief.

I focused all my attention on my daughter. When the quadruped first came sniffing on padded paws I was oblivious, so lost was I in my daughter's struggle. A shaggy, smelly thing, in itself it was no threat, but we knew that its master would not be far behind. I peered through the dark for any sign of life in my daughter. I could see none.

The strange melody was repeated several times, ending as the first light of dawn topped the cinder cone Again, silence was interrupted only by the sounds of the animal.

As the yellow sun rose above the horizon, coloring the clouds with pink, my husband sighed. He reached down, gathered some of the fungi, and pocketed it. The master called to the quadruped. It vocalized in return.

Still concealed in cloaking, my husband signaled my son. Too weak to carry his sister, my son grabbed her cloak and tossed it over her body as my husband clamped a strong hand over my mouth, trapping my scream within me. He dragged me away. I dissolved into the abyss of my agony.

Susie Watkins's Story

The dark was thick, with no moon and shifting cloud cover muting the starlight. Red light from my headband helped me adjust my vision between the ground and the night sky. As I moved, the light slid along, glowing bloody on the hard, barren surface below my feet and the scattered, straggly plant life.

For a moment I thought my eye caught movement near a stand of juniper about fifty yards away. I assumed it was a skunk or a bobcat on the prowl, but my bloodhound companion Bo didn't alert, so I figured

I was wrong. Wind rushing through a nighthawk's wings creating a startling boom. I stumbled, jostling the pipes in my backpack. Nerves, I decided. Earlier when I checked in at the office, I dismissed that UFO freak in the parking lot without a second thought. He shoved his card at me, demanding that I report any sightings. My curt retort, "I'm not a believer," was cut short by his rejoinder, "You will be!"

His words planted seeds in my mind that were sprouting as I made my way along a silent path. The impossible possibility, casually rejected in the light of day, reared its worrisome visage in the dark of night. I wasn't scared, of course, because I didn't believe, but . . .

I was a musician/photographer artist-in-residence at Craters of the Moon National Preserve, Idaho, United States of America, Earth. Craters, so like the desolation of our moon, isn't for everyone. NASA sends astronauts here to train, and occasionally they leave behind a bit of advanced technology, or so I'd been told. Anyway, for me it was just perfect. A very long time ago, lava flows had cooled and hardened on the surface while hotter lava continued to flow below, forming natural caves. These caves, known as lava tubes, served as my laboratory and studio. In one particular tube, a stalactite joined with a stalagmite to form a column, nearly blocking the entire cave and distorting sound as it split into different speeds flowing around the obstacle.

Daytime sounds of curious explorers and hikers oblivious to my need for silence complicated my work, so I became a night owl, working from around ten o'clock to dawn. Tonight was bagpipe night. I got the microphone situated on the far side of the barrier and set up my recording equipment. As soon as I pulled my bagpipes from the pack, Bo issued a silent reproach with his sad bloodhound eyes. Even his loyalty had its limits. He moseyed back to the cave entrance.

On previous nights the lava tubes had distorted my oboe music, creating a sound I was sure was unique in all the world. The night photography on the stark lava flow outstripped everything I'd come up with before. I was sure my music and photography would make a surreal artistic experience when they were combined into an immersive 3D exhibit.

I could go into detail about my recording equipment and the vibrations and shadows in the tubes, but that is not this story. Suffice it to say that the environment is weird and the echoes of sound strangely warped.

As the sun rose and the clouds lit up a delicate pink, I left the cave with my equipment and drew in a deep breath of the moist, cool air. I saw Bo playing near two juniper bushes. “Bo, what are you doing?”

Bo acknowledged my call with a deep “woof” and looked in my direction, but took not one step toward me. Instead, the old bloodhound pasted his nose to the ground and followed a scent around the junipers. In a minute or two he began whipping his head up and down and back and forth. Then he dropped to the ground and rubbed his body in the dirt from nose to tail, trying to rid himself of whatever was bothering him. We had already done the skunk bath treatments once this summer. I fervently hoped my old dog had learned that lesson. “Bo! Beauregard! Come on, boy, it’s time for breakfast.”

Still, he did not obey. That meant something was wrong. Breakfast was a high priority for my old bloodhound.

I trudged down the hill with my pipes clattering in my backpack. I was relieved not to smell the distinctive defense of a black-and-white night prowler. Bo’s head was hidden in the bushes; all I could see of him was his tail. I stretched my right arm, reaching for his collar, when something touched my left hand. With Bo’s collar secured in my grasp, I closed my free fingers around what felt like cloth and gave it a pull. Bo’s body had been hidden not by the brush but by the fabric I grasped in my fingers. It was lightweight, as large as a cloak for an adult, and invisible.

For a moment we shared a confused look. I explored the fabric with both hands. It felt silky smooth and light as air. I turned it over and shifted it in the morning light, but all I could see was the brush beyond it. Bo sniffed at it, but then another scent caught his nose, and he hurried away in his arthritic trot. I stood for a moment, mystified by what I held. Maybe the astronauts had left behind a new camouflage technology?

Bo sounded, letting me know he had located the source of the scent. I tucked the mystery of the camouflaging cloth into a corner of my mind and wrapped the large swath of material around me. I got disoriented for a moment because I could not see my legs and feet but, after a few tentative steps, I regained confidence and struck out to see what else Bo had found.

He was pawing at something hidden in a hollow at the base of a juniper bush. I dropped the invisible material to the ground and knelt to see what enticed my bloodhound to this particular spot.

When I first looked into the hole, shock knocked me onto my butt. After a breathless moment, I rubbed my eyes and shook my head. Curiosity got the better of me, and I got on my knees to get a closer look. I blinked several times to be sure I was seeing what I was seeing. Nestled among the roots of the Junipers was a—well, a child of sorts. At least the general form was that of a three-year-old of my own kind. Bo thrust his nose into the child's face. He inhaled the scent of our new discovery, looked up at me, and licked my cheek. It was his "can we keep it?" look. I pushed him aside.

The young face captivated me. Short downy blond feathers covering the top of her head gleamed in the beams of the rising sun. A pert little nose with only one nostril and a sweet little bow of a mouth pulled into a pucker were framed in skin of palest yellow. But it was her direct gaze into my eyes that formed an instant bond. At first the eyes seemed quite like my own in form, but as they adjusted to the light, I noted that the amber iris and the dark pupil were not round, but hexagonal.

Her hand brushed a bare patch of skin on the side of her head. Maybe an ear? She held my gaze. Her head tilted to one side. Then she reached out to me in the irresistible, universal gesture of the very young.

I gathered her into my arms. She was unexpectedly light, causing me to lose my balance and rock onto my butt again. The sudden movement seemed to delight the child, who gave me a toothless grin. I wrapped her in the invisible fabric and, with Bo at my side, carried her to my cabin. The sky changed to prophetic red, and storm clouds gathered on the horizon. As we reached the porch, raindrops tapped a gentle rhythm on the metal roof.

In the cabin I laid the little one on the bed. Her mouth opened and closed repeatedly. Her eyes followed me. I offered a drink of water. She drained the whole cup in large gulps. I gave her some bread and she nibbled at it. I tried a dried beef strip, but she pushed that to the floor where Bo promptly gobbled it up. Both looked delighted. Bo wagged, and the child, who still hadn't made a sound, held out her hands for more.

With no internet or phone service near my cabin, my car a half day's hike back to the parking lot, and a deluge in the making, I was at a loss about what to do next. My little guest and my dog suffered no such qualms. The child pulled the strange textile into a nest around her and drifted off to sleep with Bo snuggled next to her.

I sat studying this new creature. She posed no threat, of that I was sure. What was she? Where did she come from? What would become of her once the world knew of her?

I lay down next to them. It had been a long night, and under the lulling spell of the rain, I gave into fatigue and slept.

I woke to the sound of a downpour pounding on the roof. The child and Bo were both gone, and the door was wide open. Wiping sleep from my eyes, I went to the porch. Bo and the child danced in the rain. Not playing fetch or chasing each other around, but dancing in a rhythmic pattern of steps, slides, twirls, and leaps with rain running down their faces.

I picked up my banjo and played along with their rhythm from the porch. The child whistled, repeating each phrase of "Rain, Rain, Go Away." I tried something more complex, and she kept right up. Finally, I tried "Dueling Banjos," a challenge song in which one player sets a tune and the other repeats it with the tempo increasing on each round. The young dancer stopped in acceptance of my challenge. Up on toes, with legs apart and arms spread wide, she looked directly at me and whistled each phrase I played. Faster and faster I lobbed variations of the tune, and she answered faster and faster until I had to concede. I bowed. The child danced away, improvising new tunes and adding new steps. That's when I knew I would be calling her Melody.

I decided that there was no hurry in notifying the world of Melody's existence. Taking her to the authorities would interrupt my work. And, most importantly, Bo and I were enjoying having our unique little friend to ourselves. Over the next week, Melody grew with astounding speed. She loved fruit and seeds and never had enough water. Melody abhorred meat, which Bo accepted with doleful gratitude. Strength in her legs and arms increased to the point I thought she might launch into flight from one of her dancing leaps. When the sun shone, Melody stayed quiet in the shadows, but when the dark clouds gathered, she exploded into whistles and dance. Bo seemed to empathize with her mood, ignoring his arthritis to join in her antics. Other times Melody stared at the horizon and softly whistled a mournful, soulful, lonely tune that made Bo howl.

Every day I practiced getting a song just right on one of my musical instruments. Every night I packed up my equipment and headed for the lava tube with Melody and Bo in tow. Tonight was flute night. This time I planned to record the same song I played on the bagpipes a week earlier: "Amazing Grace."

Melody and Bo played around the entrance to the cave. When I took a break to check on them, they had settled into her invisible cloaking to snooze. I had completed a really good session and turned off my equipment when I heard Melody whistling. There was a whole new tenor to her song. She was agitated, excited, calling out. I ran toward the entrance. Melody and Bo were halfway down the cinder path headed for the juniper bushes.

As I closed the distance between us, Bo let out a yelp and a moan. His arthritis had locked his hind legs. He scooted along, trying to keep up with Melody.

I dropped down next to Bo. "It's okay," I comforted. "I'll get her. You stay here and rest."

Bo kept his failing eyes locked on Melody, probably more through scent than vision. The cataracts wouldn't allow him to see very far in the faint light of dawn leaking over the mountain.

I rose and looked down the path to the juniper. Melody was running madly toward the bushes. I caught my toe and stumbled. When I looked up again, she was gone. The birds in the juniper made a ruckus and flew away in a mad flurry.

Melody suddenly appeared and ran to my arms. Behind her my view of the juniper rippled and dissolved to reveal a small group of adults who looked just like Melody. The same yellow feathers and skin, the long skinny legs and arms. Her family.

Melody led me by the hand toward the small group as they continued to whistle back and forth. One adult wrapped me in a warm embrace, then placed her forehead against mine. The others placed their hands on my back and my shoulders. A feeling of deep gratitude flowed into me.

Behind me I heard the thunder of a helicopter. Flashing red and blue lights momentarily preceded emergency vehicles racing down the mountain toward us. Sirens shrieked. The crack of a gunshot split the air.

The family pulled a couple of junipers out of the ground where they had been digging. Melody's mom grabbed her. The whole group started running for the top of the cinder cone, disappearing into their cloaking as they ran. I felt helpless watching the events unfold. Bo dragged himself to my side and crumpled to the ground.

Bright lights appeared in the sky, shining down onto the top of the cinder cone. Then those lights went out. There was no sign of Melody and her family. The sirens fell silent. The helicopter disappeared over the horizon.

I plopped down next to Bo as emergency vehicles roared by. A truck dropped off one helmeted gunman who stood over me commanding, "Don't move." He was scared, really scared. I could hear it in his voice. I didn't move.

The convoy returned. Bo and I were loaded into a Jeep, then I was transferred into a van. A soldier carried Bo away. I called after them, "My dog needs pain medication. It's in my cabin. His arthritis is bad. He needs a pill."

Over hours of interrogation in the van, my fear and sad confusion turned to anger, then outrage. I stopped even trying to answer the barrage of questions. Instead, I hummed "Amazing Grace" over and over. At last, a soldier let me out and escorted me across the parking lot to my car. My belongings and equipment filled the back of my little hatchback. The sun was setting, and my memories of the day's occurrences were becoming confused, when a man with a lot of brass on his uniform ordered me to go home and keep quiet. Behind him Bo was giving me a big grin and attempting to wag from the backseat of my vehicle. I was sure he was laughing at the shiny clown roaring at me.

The young man who had held me at gun point—he couldn't have been more than nineteen—told me, "We were real gentle with your dog, ma'am. We even gave him the pain medication."

"Thanks," I replied, functioning on autopilot. I insisted on checking the equipment and found that my microphone was missing. "I need that mic. It was expensive. Can't I just take a few minutes to go by the cave and pick it up?"

The young soldier looked around as he closed the back of the car. "I guess it won't do any harm. I'll drive."

The process of taking inventory and the ride to the cave gave my mind time to clear. At the mouth of the cave, I let Bo out for a stretch—we had a long drive home ahead of us. I went directly to the back of the cave and retrieved my mic. When I returned, I noticed Bo curled into the spot where he and Melody had slept the night before. I gathered him and the invisible fabric up and carried them to the back seat. I was ready to leave this rocky moonscape behind.

When we reached the boundary of the park and my car was pointed toward the highway, the soldier told me, "Sarge says to tell you we're sorry about the inconvenience, but for your own good don't talk about what happened here." His face fell. His voice trembled as he urged me,

"Really, ma'am, please, don't talk about it. Folks just aren't that woke. We're not ready."

A few weeks later, I was home editing video and music recordings with Bo sleeping at my feet in a blanket that would have been invisible if not for the dog hair covering it. My work was interrupted when my computer shut down and rebooted, displaying a message from Melody's mom. It contained the information that is presented at the beginning of this writing as "Nu-A-P-P's Story."

I dug out that parking lot UFO guy's card and emailed a link to "I'm a Believer," the old Monkees song revived by the movie Shrek.

From the message on my computer, I learned that our intergalactic neighbors named the people of Earth after two space exploration probes we launched back in 1977. Their people captured the probes and learned about us from the electronics in the ship's computers. I leave you with an important message written by Melody's mom Nu-A-P-P.

Greetings, Voyagers,

We are unharmed. We took from your home only that which we needed to save our people.

It is evident that you have prepared to defend your planet and to engage in destructive behavior to ward off enemies. The individual Voyager my family encountered showed a capacity for empathy and behavior conducive to peaceful and mutually profitable transactions. But it is obvious that your leadership is not prepared for peace and trade with those different from yourselves.

Voyagers, be aware that we are not alone. Others will come visiting. You are on the brink of a new beginning. Prepare for the future you want.

Nu-A-P-P

Carol McManus
The Reunion

CASSIE BALANCED THE TRAY HOLDING THREE CRYSTAL champagne flutes, a bottle of Dom Perignon P2 2000, and her fresh-out-of-the-oven bacon-wrapped chestnuts. She placed it on the glass-top wicker table in front of Joan and Vivian. Her best friends from childhood were perched on the porch swing while the warm summer breeze moved through the trees. It felt good to be home.

Joan's eyes widened. "Where did you unearth that champagne? It's harder to find than truffles in a corn field."

Cassie winked at her friend. "Where there's a will, there's a way." She removed the foil and pointed the bottle over the railing toward the yard before popping the cork with her thumb.

"You did that with the artistry of a Master Sommelier. I'm impressed. I remember when you couldn't get a twist cap off a bottle of beer." Vivian leaned forward and grabbed two cocktail napkins, positioning a warm canapé on each before handing one to Joan and lifting the other to her mouth. "You don't mind if we start, do you?" she asked after she swallowed the bite.

"Of course not. Eat them while they're hot." Cassie managed to fill all three glasses without champagne bubbling over the side.

"I don't know about you two, but while calls, texts, and emails are fine, it's so much better when we're together in person."

Returning the bottle to the tray, Cassie picked up two flutes and handed them to Joan and Vivian, then lifted hers in the air. "Ladies, a toast. Here's to our sixtieth birthdays. May we live long and prosper."

"Here's to decades of love and laughter," Joan added.

"And here's to a lifetime of memories that started right here on this porch." Vivian tipped her glass, and they clinked before taking their first sip of the rich, creamy bubbly.

"One of our professors is a statistical genius and he says the odds of three people in a school district the size of ours in little old Dallas, PA, sharing the same birthday are astronomical. He even told me the formula, but I don't remember." Joan pointed her index finger at Cassie and Vivian, then at herself. "But here we are."

"Do you think that's what drew us together, or was it something else?" Vivian mused.

Joan spoke first. "We can't forget singing in the youth choir at church and endless hours dedicated to 4-H activities."

Cassie popped a bacon delight into her mouth before settling into the empty wicker chair. "Shit. Look at us. Three girls who grew up in rural Pennsylvania, all part of the family businesses: one milking cows and baling hay, one picking apples in the orchards, and the other loading, unloading, and arranging furniture at the Morgans' store in town. Who knew on the eve of our sixtieth birthdays we'd be sitting on the same front porch where we used to pluck feathers off chickens?"

"You forgot to mention fifty years later drinking a five-hundred-dollar bottle of champagne on that porch." Vivian grabbed two more bites from the plate and stuffed both in her mouth.

Joan nodded. "My daddy always said, 'Early to bed and early to rise—'"

"We know, we know," Cassie interrupted, "'—makes a man healthy, wealthy, and wise.'"

Joan drained her glass. "Well I, for one, am not at all surprised. After all, look how our lives unfolded. My brothers took over the orchard business, and Viv's sister and brother-in-law are still selling furniture. We were the lucky ones. We were determined to get out of here and make something of ourselves, and by God, we did."

"It is kind of funny that for this reunion we traded in plane tickets and fancy clothes for good old-fashioned sweatshirts and faded jeans."

Vivian tucked a stray lock of her long silver hair behind her ear. "Is this called coming full circle?"

"Are you saying a leopard never changes its spots?" Cassie asked.

Joan responded. "I think what she's saying is the grass isn't always greener on the other side of the fence."

Vivian took a sip. "I don't know about you, but I did a helluva lot of mowing, watering, and fertilizing of that so-called green grass."

Cassie almost blew champagne out of her nose. "I think it's time for the girls from Dallas High to stand up and review who we were and how far we've come. After all, it's tradition. We've done this on every ten-year milestone since we were ten years old. Vivian, you go first."

Vivian stood and walked to the opposite end of the porch before making a dramatic turn and facing her cohorts. "Ladies, I would like to start our walk down memory lane with that party our moms threw for three little girls on their first double-digit birthday nearly fifty years ago. Do you remember how cool it felt to be turning ten? We thought we were so grown up. In fact, I think it was the first time any of us wore dresses except to go to church."

Cassie nodded. "I remember mama bringing us a pitcher of iced tea and fresh baked chocolate chip cookies. She almost dropped the tray when she heard us saying we could now wear stockings and use makeup. Her exact words were, 'Just don't forget to wear clean underwear in case you're in an accident.' I never did figure out what that had to do with stockings and makeup, but I admit I never leave home without my clean underwear."

Joan burst out laughing. "Your mom had a bushelful of sage advice, and she loved to share it whenever she had the chance."

"I call them my earworms of youth," Cassie said, laughing. "It's amazing to me how many of those sayings come out of my mouth even today."

"Don't interrupt," Vivian scolded. "I wasn't finished." She pulled three folded pieces of yellowed paper from her pocket and handed one to Cassie and one to Joan, keeping the third for herself. "Our tradition at these reunions is to read aloud what dreams for the future we wrote about on our tenth birthdays."

"I thought we agreed to lose those after our fiftieth birthday get-together," Cassie said.

"Yes, that was discussed, but we never agreed. So I kept them," Vivian asserted. "Joan, you first."

Joan's auburn hair shone in the afternoon sun. Her green eyes shimmered, and she took another sip of champagne before she began. "I, Joan Simpson, hereby declare that when I grow up, I want to travel to a faraway place. I will marry a prince and he'll make me his princess. And we'll live in a beautiful castle with servants who will pick the apples so I never have to do it again."

"I remember the time you fell off the ladder in the orchard. I think you were eight or nine." Cassie stretched her long slender legs out in front of her.

"And don't forget the time you broke your arm when it got caught in a branch. When you dropped to the ground, you landed right in a bushel of apples." Vivian elbowed Joan. "I guess an apple a day doesn't always keep the doctor away."

"You know, I'd give anything to pick a fresh apple from one of those trees and bite into the juicy flesh. I didn't know how good I had it back then." Joan wiped away a tear.

Vivian nodded. "Your grandma's pies were the best." She turned to Cassie. "You're next."

"Okay, here goes." She unfolded her paper. "I, Cassie Miller, do hereby declare I'll buy all the surrounding farms and then I can have a hundred horses. And I'll be a champion rider with rooms full of ribbons, awards, and trophies. And I'll have dozens of dogs, and they'll have puppies I can give away to make lonely kids happy."

Joan laughed. "The phrase that comes to mind is, 'Don't count your chickens before they hatch.' That one sure didn't come true."

"No judgment, remember?" Vivian snapped. "Our rule is to share our little girl dreams at every ten-year birthday celebration so we can remember those times together—but without regret."

Cassie gazed out at the pastures and pointed to the concrete slab surrounded by the still-scarred earth. "Remember, the barn stood right there. After grandma and grandpa passed, mom and dad tried to keep the farm going, but a hundred acres just wasn't big enough to compete. Maybe if I'd had siblings, things would have been different. But Frank and I were living in Connecticut, and we were immersed in growing our business. He hated the rural life." She turned back to the girls. "Then when the barn burned down and they lost the cows, they saw it as a sign to give up."

"But the pastures are in beautiful shape. What happened when your parents retired to Florida?"

Cassie shook her head. "They weren't ready to sell so they leased the fields to one of the only remaining farmers in the area, and I pay someone to maintain the house. This is the first time I've been back in a couple of years, and nothing has changed. It's time for the next chapter."

"Do you want to talk about it, Cassie?" Joan leaned forward and divided the rest of the champagne between the glasses.

"No. Things will look better in the morning." She brightened. "Viv, it's your turn. We haven't heard your ten-year-old dreams."

Vivian scanned her paper in silence before she started to read. "I, Vivian Morgan, will grow up to be rich and beautiful. I'll live in a big mansion, and I'll have a dozen kids. My husband will be smart and handsome, and I will fill our home with beautiful furniture just like my daddy sells in his store."

"Oh, I do remember your family's furniture store. I think I was six or seven when my mom wanted to buy a new sofa. I sat on every sofa and chair in the time it took for her to make up her mind. And do you know, they still have that same sofa. It's the only piece they took when they moved into the retirement village near Lancaster."

"I guess that's an example of, 'Don't throw the baby out with the bathwater.'" Cassie teased.

"Now you're just doing it on purpose. You and your earworms!" Joan stood and picked up the tray and headed for the door. "Cassie, I don't know what you have cooking in the oven but it smells divine, and I'm thinking it's time to move this party inside."

"Oh, crap! I forgot all about dinner." Just then the timer went off in the kitchen.

"Some things never change. You'd forget your head if it wasn't attached." Vivian emptied her glass and followed Joan and Cassie inside.

***

Over a sumptuous dinner of short ribs, mashed potatoes, and fresh steamed broccoli, the women caught up on recent events in their lives.

Joan shared tales of tutoring grad students whose heads were so high in the academic clouds they had no clue about the real world. "I know you probably think I'm the same way, but at least I had experience in the family business growing up."

Cassie brought tears to everyone's eyes with her stories of teams of lawyers trying to settle the sale of her business. "This one in particular wore a very expensive Armani suit to every meeting. Problem was, he must have been forty pounds lighter when he purchased it and I couldn't help staring at his one remaining button, waiting for it to pop."

Vivian shared stories of life in the suburbs with vapid socialites. "I was horrified when I heard one say, 'I just don't understand how any woman can work. I'm much too busy playing tennis and managing our social calendar.' I can't believe I existed in that world for so long."

The comfortable discourse lasted almost two hours before they moved to the living room with plates of Cassie's warm bread pudding smothered in whiskey sauce.

"I'm thinking it's time for some brandy to go with our dessert. Any takers?"

"That's a great idea, Joan. There's a bottle of Courvoisier XO in the bar, and the snifters are on the shelf."

"Viv, I assume you want to partake?" Joan didn't wait for an answer.

She placed three glasses on the bar and retrieved the Cognac from the cabinet.

When all three had their glasses in hand, Cassie spoke. "Fifty years ago, if anyone told me I'd be celebrating my sixtieth birthday in the house I grew up in with my BFFs from childhood, I'd have told them they were crazy. But here we are. Three old broads who've been through it all and we're here to tell the story."

"Hey, hey. There's no old broads in this room—only three sensational, slightly mature women," Joan protested.

"Hear, hear!" Vivian took a swig of her brandy and coughed. She clamped her eyes shut and pressed her lips together, suppressing a sneeze.

"You need some water?" Cassie started to rise.

Vivian waved her back into her seat. "And dilute all this good alchohol? Hic! Oops. I mean alcohol."

"C'mon, girls. It's time to fish or cut bait. We need to pick up the pace. We've only reviewed our tens. Let's move on to the year we turned twenty." Joan kicked off her shoes and settled back in the overstuffed recliner.

Vivian stared at Joan. "Are you testing us? I'm going to start counting how many times we use those old pearls of country wisdom." She spread her hands in front of her. "At least I would if I could feel my fingers so I could count."

"I remember when we met for our twentieth birthday. I couldn't play basketball my junior year at UConn because of my injury, and I was afraid I was going to lose my scholarship and not be able to finish school," Cassie said. "You guys were so great. We met in New York and stayed at your teeny, tiny fourth-floor walk-up, Joan. You said if they kicked me out, I could come live with you and audit classes at Columbia."

"And I said there was no way UConn was going to risk losing their star player, and I was right. You were back on the court your senior year and they won the NCAA championship because of you." Vivian slapped her knee.

"It wasn't all me, but I did play, and we did win. And I graduated with my degree in marketing and finance. I was ready to move back home, and then I met Frank." Cassie moved the tip of her finger around the rim of her glass.

"And look where that got you," Joan nodded.

Cassie snorted. "You mean what didn't kill me made me stronger?"

"If I'm not mistaken, you and Frank had some pretty good years building that tech company. He couldn't have done it without you." Vivian wagged her finger at Cassie.

"I guess you're right, but we were never able to have children. All we did was work, and then when we sold it to Broadcom, I got my half of 60 million dollars and Frank got his divorce and moved to the Bahamas with his young bimbo. I guess a million a year for thirty years of my life is reasonable. So what you're telling me is, I shouldn't cry over spilt milk." The bitterness in Cassie's voice cut through the air.

"No pity party here. Look what you can do with all that money. You're set for life, and if you ask me, you're better off without Frank."

"Viv's right, but let's not jump ahead. We have a few more birthdays to cover. I'd like to talk about our thirtieth birthday reunion. That was when everything changed for me."

"Go ahead, Joan. All I remember about that year was trolling every bar and honky-tonk in Nashville and being drowned out by mind-numbing country music." Cassie stepped to the bar to refill her glass. "You ready for more?"

"Fill her up. I want Joan to tell us again about what happened when she met Peter," Vivian urged.

"That was the year—and Nashville, of all places. Peter was there for a conference, and his buddies dragged him to the same bar that night. I bumped his elbow on my way to the ladies' room and his drink drenched the front of his shirt. One of his buddies jumped up like he was going to punch me. And for reasons I'll never understand, I said, 'If you keep making that face, it'll freeze that way.'"

Cassie interjected. "Now that is the voice of your mother."

Joan continued. "I walked away and never saw him again. That is, until I spent the summer at the Ozette Native American Village as part of the archaeological dig. My parents were so disappointed when I majored in art history. They scrimped and saved to send me to Columbia, so sure I'd study management or finance. You know, something practical so I could take over the furniture store and grow the business."

"You're drifting, Joan. Back to the good part," Vivian insisted.

"If I recall, you were teaching at the time," Cassie said.

"Sort of. Columbia hired me as a graduate teaching assistant. It was a way to start working on my master's degree since my parents were no longer footing the bill. I can remember Pop saying, 'When you start paying the bills, you can do whatever you want.'" Joan sighed. "When I saw the posting for the dig in Washington, I jumped at the chance to go during my summer break. I always wanted to be an archaeologist."

"And that's where you met Peter again." Vivian urged her along.

Joan nodded. "Yes, I didn't know it, but he was a professor at Columbia, teaching archaeology in their graduate program. I knew the name, but I had no idea it was the same guy I spilled a drink on in Nashville—not until we both ended up in Washington at that dig."

"Blah, blah, blah. Get to the good part." Cassie giggled.

Joan obliged. "We fell in love. We got married six weeks later right there at the dig site. I gave up my loft, and the rest is history. And we both still have a love-hate relationship with country music!"

"Not so fast. You left out raising two beautiful boys, both of whom graduated college with honors and are happily married with kids of their own. I guess there really is a lid for every pot. And before you say anything, that one comes from my grandmother." Vivian stood. "Anybody besides me got the munchies? Cassie, do you have any popcorn in the house?"

"Of course. In the pantry. Bowls are in the bottom cabinet next to the fridge. While you nuke it, I'm heading to the little girls' room." Cassie drained her snifter and headed down the hall.

Vivian called from the kitchen. "Should I start a pot of coffee?"

"No!" Cassie shouted. "The party is just getting started."

While they were gone, Joan went to the bar and pulled out the Tito's vodka and Kahlua. She called to Vivian. "When you come back, bring some ice. If we're going to talk about our fortieth get-together, we're gonna need some Black Russians."

"Uh-oh," Cassie said when she returned. "Looks like we're moving on to Las Vegas."

"Damn straight." Vivian was holding her new drink and handed one to Cassie. "Forty was my year. You two were married and happy, and I was living the Stepford Wife life in New Canaan, Connecticut. Las Vegas was my idea. I had to get away and have some fun."

"I never understood that," Cassie said. "Our lives seemed so tame; me working alongside Frank to build his tech company—"

Joan interrupted. "And me raising the boys and teaching part-time at Columbia while Peter kept racking up degrees. You lived the glamorous life."

"Oh yes, it was glamorous all right. Nothing but fancy parties, country club, expensive trips with Nathan's clients, and a daughter who spent half her year at boarding school in Switzerland. I was going mad because I had lost who I was." Vivian pulled a tissue from her pocket and blew her nose.

"I never did believe that every cloud has a silver lining," Cassie consoled.

"You guys know I never finished my psychology degree at Penn because I started working to support Nathan so he could get his degree in finance. La-di-da. He went on to be a hotshot investment banker on Wall Street, and I was the dutiful wife."

"Sorry Viv, but dutiful wives don't wrap their legs around poles to the tune of 'Bootylicious.' I'm still amazed we didn't get arrested that night." Joan swirled the Black Russian before dipping her tongue in the dark liquid.

Cassie jumped in. "Now let's be fair, Joan. It wasn't all Viv that night. I seem to recall you tipping your elbow a few too many times and passing out on the dance floor."

Joan laughed. "We were badasses that year. What was so special about turning forty?"

Vivian stuck out her bottom lip. "I think it was the realization that it could be the halfway point in our lives, and we hadn't done the things we dreamed of doing when we were ten."

Joan raised her hand. "Ooh, ooh! I've got a good earworm for that one. 'If at first you don't succeed, try, try again.'"

"Maybe," Cassie mused, "but we were all successful in our own way. After all, we got away from smelly cows, rotten orchards, and long retail hours. We did pretty well for ourselves."

"But none of us achieved the dreams of those ten-year-old girls. Cassie, what happened to your dreams of being a champion equestrian? And Joan, when did you trade servants picking apples for musty books and boring lectures?"

Joan's eyes sparkled with unshed tears. "Come on, Viv, you're looking at this all wrong. Truth is, you're the one who came closest to those dreams. You got your mansion and your house full of beautiful furniture."

"I suppose you're right. I didn't have a dozen kids, but I have a beautiful, successful daughter who's happily married and has blessed me with three adorable grandchildren. But losing Nathan left a big hole in my heart. Damn him for choosing a career that put him in an early grave. He couldn't handle the stress and his heart gave out. Truth is, I wish I could go to one more company party with him just to savor the moment when he'd wink at me from across the room. That was our signal that it was time to go home and head for the bedroom."

Cassie and Joan joined Viv on the sofa, and the women embraced. Joan whispered, "How utterly delicious. I know you miss him every day, Viv."

"Has it really been ten years since Nathan died? Our fiftieth birthday certainly wasn't a traditional reunion, but we were together. We mourned with you, Viv." Cassie lifted Vivian's chin. "Do you remember what you said after the funeral and what we promised each other that day?"

Vivian nodded. "I do. I remember we said the half-century mark was only the beginning of the second half of our lives. And the next fifty were going to be even better. It was hard to imagine then."

Joan asked, "And have they been?"

They laughed and nodded.

Cassie took the lead. "Frank may be gone with his young trophy, but I realize I don't need him or any other man to make my life whole. I'm free now, and I have the money to do whatever I want. The little girl who dreamed about horses is alive and well, even if her dreams have changed over the years."

"Bravo, Cassie," Joan said. "As for me, that girl who wanted a castle and servants realizes that her deep love is for those musty books and a dusty old husband. Our lives may be boring to some, but he still makes her heart flutter. I can't wait until Peter returns from his summer expedition to Egypt. I'm thinking I may have to join him next year. It's been too long."

Vivian perked up. "And I have an announcement to make."

"Do tell." Joan's eyebrows lifted.

The grandfather clock in the hall struck midnight.

"Wait. Hold that thought." Cassie stood. "Ladies, I believe it is a new day, and a very special day as I recall." A broad smile spread across her face.

Joan picked up on her cue. "You're right. It's midnight, and you know what that means."

Vivian sniffed. "Oh God. Are we officially sixty years old today?"

"We are, and we came here to celebrate." Cassie disappeared to the kitchen and returned in a flash with another chilled bottle of Dom Perignon P2 2000 and three glasses.

Once the glasses were filled, Cassie turned to Vivian. "Now, young lady, what's the announcement?"

Vivian took a long drink of her champagne before setting it down on the table. She stood and walked to the fireplace before turning back to her friends. "I'm getting married!"

"What?" Cassie shouted.

"Why did you wait so long to tell us?" Joan demanded.

Vivian beamed. "Because I wanted it to be my birthday present to my best friends."

"We're so happy for you. Tell us everything." Cassie refilled their glasses for another toast.

Vivian said, "All in good time. Tradition dictates that as soon as the clock turns, we each share a new beginning. Joan, what's yours?"

"I guess this is kind of a big deal, but in September I will be a full professor at Columbia. I finished my PhD last year."

"And you kept this a secret?" Cassie chided. "How long have you known?"

"A few months, but I didn't want to share on one of our phone calls. I wanted to tell you in person." Joan let out a deep breath. "Now come on, Viv. Dish."

"I met him at church. He's a widower and a real estate attorney. How boring is that? And oh, by the way, his heart is stronger than an ox. And here's the kicker: he wants me to go back to school to finish my degree. Can you believe it, after all these years? Guess you don't always have to be the early bird to catch the worm."

Cassie shook her head. "Joan, Vivian, I'm so happy for both of you. I'm not sure my new beginning rises to the level of your announcements."

"Well don't keep us in suspense. What's your news?" Vivian urged.

"I just put in an offer for the adjoining 200 acres. I'm moving back home."

Joan erupted. "That's wonderful! And now you'll finally have your horses?"

"Sort of. I'm starting a nonprofit rescue farm for animals. Details to follow."

* * *

Sunday morning after brunch, Joan and Vivian loaded up their cars. They exchanged hugs and were about to leave when Cassie stopped them. "Whoever said blood is thicker than water didn't know the girls from Pennsylvania. Ladies, I have a new tradition that I'd like to propose. We're not getting any younger—"

"Speak for yourself," Vivian chided.

"Hear me out. I think we should celebrate every year from here on. The cards and calls in between have worked fine in the past, but I don't want another ten years to go by before we get together again. What do you say? Next year? Here? I'll have the champagne on ice." She waited.

"I can't think of a better new tradition," Joan answered. "And I'm going to start researching earworms. I wouldn't be surprised if some of them originated thousands of years ago and I'll uncover them on my next dig."

"I'll send you invitations to the wedding. Just warning you—you may have to take a ski lift to the top of a mountain to be part of the ceremony!" Vivian hugged Cassie and Joan one more time.

Cassie waved as they drove away. "Here's to new beginnings!"

Susan Martha Thompson
Why the Roadrunner Runs

"ALL I CAN PICTURE IN MY MIND IS THE ROADRUNNER being chased by a coyote in the cartoons I watched when I was a kid," Chelsey's grandmother stated. She squinted her eyes and tilted her head.

"What do you mean, Granny?" Chelsey asked.

"Well," Granny continued, "in this cartoon, a coyote was always going after a roadrunner. He never actually caught it. No matter what happened to the bird, it always survived. And the coyote usually went off a cliff or ended up in some kind of fix. It seemed funny at the time. I was too young to know you couldn't do that and live."

"Sounds silly." Chelsey smirked and gave a huff.

"The only thing I learned from that cartoon was that coyotes aren't very smart," Granny added. "What confused me later in life was when a coyote figured out how to get into our barn to kill a bunch of our chickens with all the doors and windows shut tighter than a fiddle. Made me kinda wonder about all the other information I gathered as a kid from the stuff I watched on TV. Like folks gettin' gunned down on *Gunsmoke* and then bein' back sittin' on their front porches or drinkin' in the saloon. There they were, the next week, ready for another confrontation. Guess we believed jus' about anything back in those days."

"Granny, I don't know anything about all that, but this isn't about a cartoon. Like I told you, it's about a real roadrunner," Chelsey said, gritting her teeth. *Living here in West Virginia with Granny since Mom and Dad died in that car crash a year ago hasn't been easy. We always seem to annoy each other. She never listens to me. She's an old fogey.*

"Real, huh? Okay. If I have to, let's hear it. First, what else is it about?" Granny grumbled.

"You have to pay attention to me! Please mute the TV, Granny." Chelsey relaxed her fists. She had to concentrate so she didn't hold herself straight and stiff like she always did when getting into arguments with her grandmother. Her counselor said it isn't healthy. *This is what I hate about living here.*

"Okay, okay. Here, happy?" Granny grabbed the TV remote and hit the mute button so hard the device flipped out of her hand and onto the floor.

"Damn," she muttered out loud, grabbing the thing and tossing it on the end table. "Go on. Go on."

"My story is called, 'Why the Roadrunner Runs.'" Chelsey tried to find a comfortable position in the paisley printed overstuffed chair. *I also can't stand this chair. The fabric scratches my legs. But it's the only one near enough to Granny for her to hear me.*

"Humph. I never considered that. What made you think of something so silly? I'd really like to get back to my program. Judge Judy has a couple ding-a-lings fighting over furniture."

"I don't know." Chelsey frowned.

"All right. Might as well go on."

"It's a story from the Ishiwiki Native American tribe." Chelsey relaxed her arms and hands again. I'm going to get Granny to listen to me about something important.

"Ishi what?" Granny squinted her eyes again and shook her head.

"Ishiwiki. I made it up."

"You said this is real."

"No, I said the bird is real."

"So you, a fourteen-year-old child, have written a story you say was made up by some Indians about a bird?" Granny grinned. "Do I have to listen to this?"

"I'm not a child. I'm a teenager! And yes, I wrote this story. Can I just read it to you? Chelsey stared at the rug beneath her feet. *Maybe I don't want to read this story to Granny. Why does she have to be this way?* She sat forward in the chair and waited.

"Good grief, Girl. Go for it," Granny shouted.

"And just so you know," Chelsey added, "we had to write a story for my English class. I wanted mine to sound like one of the old Native American tales we read last week. I had some help with the wording from my teacher."

"That sounds like a smart thing to do." Granny glanced at the television and sighed.

Chelsey stood up and cleared her throat. *I'm doing this.* "First of all, I want to tell you that I learned in our geography and culture class that Native American people used, and still use, animals a lot in their stories to teach something. Native people respect animals and believe they are wise in their own ways and have a lot to teach us if we pay attention. What do you think of that, Granny?" Chelsey asked.

Granny tilted her head to the right, then to the left. She got a faraway look in her eyes. Chelsey guessed her grandmother's furrowed eyebrows meant she was thinking about something important.

"Well, I suspect they have a point," Granny said. "Living on a farm taught me over and over again how animals are smarter than we think. For example, the other culprits that liked to eat our chickens were the raccoons. We set traps out for them so we could take them miles away to live on food other than what we had to offer. Do ya think they'd go after chicken meat in the trap? Nope. Not a one. Too smart for us, they were."

"Well, here's my story about animals. Hope you like it." Chelsey began. "Why the Roadrunner Runs, by Chelsey Castelani."

> *Long ago, when the great mountains west of the Mississippi River were finally settled into themselves, the land beneath them stretched many miles, from vast green forests to dry brown sands of desert and tumbleweed. Many moons passed before the cries of roaming beasts could be heard seeking what they could for want of a meal.*

"Wait a minute. Wait a minute," Granny groused. "'For want of a meal?' You don't talk like that."

"I told you my teacher helped me. It's supposed to sound old." Chelsey glared at Granny as best she could without getting swatted.

"Okay, okay. Go on," Granny sniped.

"All right. Here goes," Chelsey started again.

The blue skies saw birds of many colors dip to earth for insects and lizards warming themselves in spring's welcome sun. After the cold desert night, many other creatures also left their burrows and homes in the rabbit brush and sage in search of breakfast. Mighty cacti reached toward the sky, offering perfect spots for nests and perching.

There was one bird, however, that spent its days roaming the land rather than mastering the winds of the air. It was silly, of course. What bird does not love to fly? This bird had a brown-and-white streaked body, small wings, very long legs, an even longer tail, and a spiky black head crest. It was not like the other birds in many ways, so much so that it wondered if it really wasn't a bird at all, but a beast that had been made to look like a bird. Try as it might, this unusual bird couldn't figure out why this had happened to it. When the great rains came and filled the arroyos, it could see in its refection that it looked like the feathered creatures above, swooping through the air and resting on cactuses. But its feelings were not heaven-bound. The long-tailed bird lurked and hunted like the beasts who slept in caves and under bushes.

"So does this critter have a name?" Granny interrupted. "What's it called? Is it the roadrunner?"

"Granny, would you please just listen to the story? Be patient. You'll find out." Chelsey gave a snort.

"Humph. Okay. Go on." Granny snorted back.

Chelsey continued.

One hot summer day, the brown bird made a decision: it would speak to creatures of the desert and ask them what they thought about its question. So off it went to seek out its friend, Desert Rat.

"Good afternoon, Desert Rat," the confused bird chirped. "Try as I may, I cannot decide if I am a creature of the air or one of the land. What do you think?"

"Oh, I believe you are much like me," Desert Rat quipped. "In spite of your many feathers, very long tail, and hard yellow beak, you chase the spiders and snakes for your dinner with your feet on the ground. Yes, for sure, you may very well even be my cousin."

"Thank you, Desert Rat," sang the brown bird. "This is good news. I'm feeling better about myself already." Off he went to speak to another friend, Little Miss Cactus Wren. He thought, It never hurts to be sure about something. Especially something as important as this.

"Hello, Miss Wren, your song is lovely. I have a question for you," said the long-tailed bird.

"Yes, it is a pretty tune, thank you. What's your question?" asked the small singer.

"I cannot decide if I am a creature of the air or of the land. I am confused regarding this matter. What do you think?" asked the brown creature.

"Oh, that's simple: you are one of the air. Have you looked at yourself? We are so much alike with our brown feathers and our streaks and spots. How could you doubt it?"

"Thank you, Miss Wren. I will consider that," muttered the large bird as it wandered away.

The bird was now more confused. It walked for a while, talking out loud. "This is not good. I don't know what to think. I will find a creature who is wise and will better understand my question. I need to talk to someone who knows what it's like to be two different animals in one." The brown bird traveled until the next day when it found another creature.

"Good morning, Mr. Salamander. I'm glad to see it's the time of year for you to be living on land. Have you found a good hole for your home?" the bird asked.

"Yes, of course. The heat of the day is much too hot on my skin. What brings you to the bank of this water?" Tiger Salamander was somewhat leery of this creature much larger than it, who had a beak that could poke and swallow it in a flash. But the bird looked so forlorn that the salamander decided to stay and find out what was troubling it.

"I am confused about myself," the long-tailed bird moaned. "My habits are those of a creature of the land, but I look like a creature of the air. I don't know what I am. I desire the freedom of the skies but find myself bound to the earth. I no longer look forward to each day as I wake. Desert Rat said one thing and Cactus Wren said another. Now I'm here hoping you can help me decide."

The salamander closed its eyes and thought. After a while it spoke. "You are a most fortunate creature," its eyes glistened. "Unlike the others, you get to understand our world in two ways rather than one."

"But, shouldn't I have to choose?" asked the bird.

"Only if you say so. But what if you decided not to choose? What if you're just something unusual but wonderful? What if you spent your days figuring out what that means?" The salamander took a deep breath in and let it out as if it were a gentle breeze.

The brown bird ruffled its feathers, flicked its tail, put its head back, and let out a loud squawk. The salamander opened its eyes and nodded its head.

Just then, a shadow came over them. The salamander and the bird both looked up to see a large creature of the air circling above them and staring down at them in a way that meant only one thing. It was breakfast time. Salamander ran toward its hole. The frightened bird ran at full speed down a path along the water, thinking how grand it was to be able to travel this way. It had seen birds of the air taken in flight by larger ones many times.

Staring straight ahead, the brown bird said a quick prayer to Creator for the salamander's safety. Back home, it rested under a large cactus to consider all it had heard from the desert animals. The bird knew that, while it looked to the skies for that feeling of freedom, being able to run on the earth had saved its life. Thinking on these matters, the bird smiled, now knowing the only decision it needed to make was to find for itself a good name.

Chelsey looked up from her page to see tears in her grandmother's eyes.

"What's wrong, Granny?" she asked.

"Oh, nothing, dear. There's a lot of wisdom in that story. You're pretty darn creative for a young'un. It kinda reminds me of something I put together a long time ago."

"Really? You like it?" Chelsey began to feel warm in her heart. It's something she wasn't used to feeling when she was with her grandmother.

"Yes, I do," Granny answered. "Ya know, your father used to write stories and poems when he was growing up. His teachers always told him he was going to become a famous writer. Later on, he got away from the writing and put all his energy into a career that would get meals on the table. Being in the Navy was his life. That, along with your mother and you. I haven't thought about that for years."

"Did he ever start writing again?" Chelsey asked.

"I don't know. He never said anything about it to me." Granny raised her eyebrows. "When he was just a kid I wrote a poem with the title, 'The Bird Who Couldn't Sing.' Would you like to hear it? If I can find it. I bet it's up in the attic in that old trunk."

"Can we go look now?" Chelsey beamed.

"Sure. Let's go." Granny grabbed the remote and shut off the TV. She gave it a stern look, shook her head, and headed toward the attic door.

* * *

"Haven't been up here in ages." Granny dusted off the top of a steamer trunk that was pushed against the far wall under a window. Opening the lid created more dust. After some mutual coughing, Granny rifled through papers and handed them to Chelsey.

"Well, here it is. Okay." With a gentler hand, Granny dusted off a nearby rocking chair for herself and a caned straight-backed chair for Chelsey. She grabbed a piece of material from the trunk and draped it over the seat of the chair so her granddaughter's legs wouldn't be pricked by the broken canes.

As they sat, Chelsey's eyes sparkled. This is going to be interesting! She lowered herself with care onto the chair, making sure to avoid the sharp pieces. She felt like she was almost holding her breath in anticipation.

Granny sat up straighter. "I really don't know why I'm doing this. I can't even remember if this is a decent poem." She cleared her throat. "Here goes. 'The Bird Who Couldn't Sing,' by Emily Castelani."

As she hopped

from branch to limb

her feathers fluffed and hollow

the tiny bird would try to sing

but not a note would follow.

She wondered if

she was so small

no music could fit in.

Was she meant to give no praise

as each day would begin?

Or welcome night

from tree tops upon high.

Instead of lullabies for sleep

her song was just a sigh.

She asked the creatures

who could sing

their tunes out loud in glory.

They laughed and said

The truth here is

you have a different story.

The melody you

give to us

and all our world to hear

is just a breath of simple joy.

The grace of it is clear.

And so the

bird so small and frail

who thought her voice was wrong

at last could hear what others knew:

She had a lovely song.

It was Chelsey's turn to have tears in her eyes. "That's really beautiful, Granny. I have a question. Are birds' bones really hollow?"

"Thank you, dear. And yes, indeed they are hollow. The little critters don't weigh much." Granny paused.

"Ya know, your story and my old poem seem to be saying a lot of the same things. They make me think I could be looking at stuff the wrong way. Especially when it comes to you. I hate to admit it, but since you came to live with me, I've felt a little like that roadrunner. I'm an old lady, set in her ways. You have all these new ideas about how to do things, and you have so much energy. Sometimes I don't know which way is up, and I feel like I'm being chased by all the responsibilities I have."

"Oh, I'm sorry, Granny." Chelsey slipped off the chair, pulling away the fabric that stuck behind her knees. "I didn't mean to make it hard for you." Tears started to travel down her cheeks. She stared into her grandmother's eyes as if she was really seeing her for the first time. "Now, dearest, none of this means I don't love you. I do. And more than you can imagine." Granny's eyes looked wetter than usual. Chelsey watched her grandmother shake her head and blink her tears away.

"Do you have any more poems?" Chelsey asked.

"I might have a couple more tucked in the trunk somewhere," Granny replied. She pondered for a moment. "But here's an idea. Would you like to try writing something together? I'd like that very much. Maybe we could do a story or a poem. What do ya think?"

"Really? Uh, that could be fun!" Chelsey felt a tingle go down her spine. "Okay then. Let's think about some ideas and we can talk about them."

Granny pulled Chelsey to her and down onto her lap. Chelsey knew her grandmother wouldn't admit that a teenager was a little heavy for her creaky bones, so she sat with the same care she showed the old chair. Granny wrapped both arms around her and kissed the side of her face.

"Perfect," Chelsey muttered. "This is what I wanted."

"It's just the first of many more," whispered Granny.

"This is what I always wanted too."

As the old woman sighed, Chelsey smiled.

Author Bios

Marylou Webster Ambrose

Marylou Webster Ambrose is an award-winning writer, editor, playwright, and actor. Her debut novel, *Your Number's Up*, a cozy comedy/mystery with a paranormal twist, is based on characters from her two-act play, *Legally Gray*, co-written with Tony Schwartz. Her humorous essays have appeared in the *Blydyn Square Review*, and her co-written plays have been performed in forty-nine states and fourteen foreign countries.

A graduate of Syracuse University School of Journalism, Marylou lives in the Pocono Lake Region of Pennsylvania with her husband Art and dog Sadie, who's a character in her novel. When she's not writing, thinking about writing, or feeling guilty for not writing, she reads inside by the fire or outside on the pontoon boat (depending on the season), experiments with gluten-free recipes, walks the dog, and overthinks.

Visit marylouambrose.com.

Dana Bree

Dana's motto is *never stop learning.*

Dana worked for NBC News in NYC as an assistant art director and along with the team, won an Emmy for design. She moved to CBS and was an associate art director for affiliate advertising. Then she moved on to public relations design, website and logo design, and publishing design.

Dana has always been an adventurer. She has a motorcycle driver's license and earned her pilot's license while living in Zimbabwe. She went skydiving with her sister and nephew over Las Vegas and traveled up the Usumacinta River in a raft in Guatemala to search out the hidden pyramids in the jungle. She traveled in the Yucatán Peninsula to explore the Mayan temples and drove across Botswana in a Land Rover to view the migrations of the wildebeest, elephants, and zebra. She is also a paranormal investigator and a dabbler in the metaphysical.

She wrote three novelettes as a ghost writer and is now creative director for Mark Victor Hansen Library. "Entering the Heart of Darkness" is the beginning of her personal story of when she lived in Africa for five years.

She loves to read, write, create, and help others publish their stories. She believes in being in the right place at the right time.

Dana Bree
stonebearpub@gmail.com
www.stonebearpublishing.com

Donna Consiglio

Donna Consiglio is a humorist who writes about what it's like to be an author. In addition to the comical and oh-so-relatable memes about not writing that she posts on social media, Donna creates whimsical notebooks and merchandise for other writers. Keep an eye out for her book entitled *I Love Writing, Not!* set to release in the near future.

New to the Sunshine State, Donna enjoys spending time on her front porch watching neighbors and wildlife as she pursues writing interactive fiction video game narratives.

She would like to travel across the country with her family in an RV so that she may get inspired to not write in some place other than her hometown.

Donna holds a master's degree in elementary education, a bachelor's degree in psychology, a handful of teaching certificates, and a plethora of course completion badges. She considers herself a lifelong learner always looking for the next course to partake in. Donna believes these are all valid excuses for *not* writing.

Laurie A. Guzda

Laurie A. Guzda is an artist, writer, and photographer. She is also an actor. In a word, she is a Storyteller.

Laurie is a seasoned improvisation actor, director, and writer. Writing sketch comedy is a favorite. She has written several screenplays, pilots, and plays. She has a monthly column called Pocono Secrets, "a discovery of what the locals know."

Laurie is the creative director of LAGuzda Creative Arts & Services, which specializes in marketing, branding, PR, and more.

www.LAGuzda.com

Elaine Leet

As a kid, Elaine Leet often thought she might have been adopted—from a distant planet. Her earliest memories are of fascination with life in all its forms and love for Earth. She finds the actions of humans quite alien, but equally interesting.

Themes common in Elaine's work include love, loss, alienation, and challenging boundaries. Reality is too strange, so she writes fiction.

Published work includes *Child of a Troubled Land* and *Chance's Diary*, along with "Ambushed," a short story published by *Grief Digest* at centering.org in 2020, and "Beware the Gray Squirrel," a poem published in *Pennsylvania Bard's Northeast Poetry Review* 2020. She won the Science Fiction Writing Award from Wayne County Library, Honesdale, Pennsylvania, in 2019.

Elaine holds a master of education degree from North Carolina Central University and professional certificates from several colleges.

Carol McManus

Carol McManus is a life-long reader and writer. Currently she holds the position of Executive Editor for the Mark Victor Hansen Library which provides ghostwriting and publishing services to clients who have a life-long dream of authoring a book.

The journey of her career spans broad geography and a broad spectrum of skills and responsibilities. After leaving a long corporate career, Carol became a coach and consultant helping small businesses and authors find their voice through branded marketing and social media. For nine years she hosted the LinkedIn Lady Show on AM and Internet radio and spoke in front of hundreds of audiences across the globe.

She lives in northeast PA with her husband, Kevin

Susan Martha Thompson

Susan is a semi-retired Licensed Professional Counselor, certified grief counselor, environmental educator and Black Hat Sect Feng Shui consultant. She has written non-published works throughout her life including a monthly newsletter, "The Natural Look;" created and produced The New World Puppetry group in which local youths performed her pro-conservation plays for schools and civic groups; developed educational presentations, performed her songs and poetry for church and camp groups; compiled group therapy materials for clients with Asperger's Syndrome and their parents and produced a document regarding culturally specific therapy while pursuing her Master's Degree. Her current work includes a children's book based on one of her plays, short stories, a literary fiction novel featuring a young Native American police officer and a book of poetry written by that character.

Susan's time spent with the Eastern Band of Cherokee of North Carolina and the Southern Ute tribe of southwestern Colorado accents her passion for the teachings of connectedness passed down by Native American Grandfathers and Grandmothers. Her stories in this book highlight their wisdom, available to all who are willing to hear.

Living in rural Northeastern Pennsylvania allows Susan time to spend hiking and exploring with her husband, Marty, and dog, Chilhowie. She enjoys stained glass work, learning to throw clay on a pottery wheel and rockhounding. Susan is an animal lover. She has rescued many kittens who matured into believing they rule the home. No one argues with them.

For comments or questions, contact Susan at:
SusanMarthaThompson@gmail.com

Mike Vreeland

Mike Vreeland is a fidgeter. Even when sitting still, his mind is all over the place with one idea or another. His writing is much the same. He's had poems and puzzles published in *Highlights for Children* magazine. His horror poems appear in the award-winning anthology *Love Letters to Poe, Vol. 1,* and in *Putrescent Poems: Horror Poetry, Vol. 1.* Other poems and short stories appear in various publications, including two in *Blydyn Square Review.* In addition, Mike has had a one-act comedy, *Wilderness Survival,* produced. And he released two CDs of original humorous children's songs, *I Sing About Things* and *Are We There Yet?* Both are now available on most streaming services.

Mike holds a master's degree in special education and certification in secondary English. Mike is a former middle school teacher and trapeze artist, but only one of those things is true.

Made in United States
North Haven, CT
01 May 2023